Love Chose Me

By: Ty Nesha

D1519443

Prologue

The Man in the Mirror

I clicked my gun off the safety before taking a long drag from my Casino. Sweat beads rolled down my forehead as I contemplated squeezing the trigger and putting an end to all my...

"What am I doing, man?" I murmured, tapping the barrel against my head.

See, I've always been one to believe that there ain't nothing that damn bad that should make a person wanna end their own life. That was for the weak, and I ain't neva been one to fold, bend or break. I stood up like a jackknife and faced the man in the mirror. Only, the man in the mirror seemed to stare back at me in contempt. He had carried so many skeletons that it had cost me everything; my family, health, and today, my sanity. I raised my gun slowly, and eventually, the cold tip of the barrel kissed my temple. I closed my eyes as my trigger finger curled naturally.

"Father, forgive me," I whispered.

Boom....

A Man Gone be a Man

I KNEW IT WOULD only be a matter of time before a multitude of nosey folks would form, and the whole block would want to know where all the commotion was coming from. But ask me if I cared. I opened my car door and stepped onto the pavement, my eyes filled with rage.

"My sister Jamel! My sister!" I screamed as I hit the driver's window with my fist. I had no idea how much strength I had mustered up until the glass shattered onto my hand.

"What in the hell is wrong wit' you, girl? You ran into my damn truck?" He countered, blocking his face with his hands.

I laughed, clearly out of my right state of mind. "My man of two years, my fiancé, just got caught screwing my sister outside *my* spot, and the first thing that comes out of your mouth is in regard to yo' whack ass ride?" I yelled as I searched my bag frantically.

"Lovey, it wasn't what you think, sis. He was just…."

My sister's eyes expanded as I pulled the small .22 from my bag. Before I could decorate my fiancés leather interior with blood, I felt a firm grasp around my wrist.

"You don't wanna do this, ma. It ain't worth it," he whispered, causing my insides to shudder.

1

TY NESHA

The sound of sirens broke my trance as I stood in the bathroom gripping the sink with my head hung low. My tears formed a never-ending melody as they hit the ceramic. I hadn't even noticed the bandage around my hand until the sharp pain screamed in protest.

"Ssss…" I cringed.

"You're lucky you don't need stitches. You did a number on yourself," a high-pitched voice sang.

"Who are you?" I asked as I walked cautiously towards her.

Her back was turned from me as her dark hair fell perfectly, stopping at the middle of her back. Confusion loomed over me as I scanned the spacious room, looking for some inkling of familiarity.

"My name is Desiree," she said, still facing the opposite direction while she fluffed the pillows on the king-size bed. "You're at the Hampton," she confirmed as I walked towards the window, admiring the view of the sun rising on Michigan Ave.

"How did I get here?" I whispered perplexedly, only recollecting bits and pieces of tonight's happenings. Regretfully, the worst part was the most vivid. I could feel a lump forming in my throat as a tear landed on the window seal.

"My brother-in-law brought you here. You were out of it when you got here, in a weird kind of daze; hadn't walked in the door good before you darted into the restroom, curled yourself into a corner, and rocked yourself into a headspace that no one but you could understand," she continued. "I told him I'd sit with you until you came to."

"You told who that?" I countered, now facing her direction.

"My brother-in-law! C.J?" She confirmed for the second time, finally turning to face me.

Her chocolate skin shone effortlessly, highlighting the nasty out-of-place bruise underneath her left eye. I walked towards her, raising my hand slowly towards her face; she grabbed my wrist firmly, stopping me in my tracks.

"Looks like you did a number on yourself as well," I indicated sincerely.

She pushed my hand away and walked around the bed to re-fluff the pillows. "I told him you can stay as long as you need. I'm not sure what you got yourself into love but…"

"How do you know my name?"

"What? Ohhhhh, your name is Love…." she said in awe as she sat at the edge of the bed.

"I didn't know that. I use the word as a term of endearment from time to time."

I watched as she smoothed out her clothes and ran her fingers through her hair. She was one of the most beautiful chocolate women I had ever seen. Her perfect figure stood out even in her loose-fitting apparel.

I could feel myself beginning to pin the blame on everything I hated about my own self. Like, maybe if I looked like her, maybe if I was thinner, prettier….

"He was gone already, girl. There was nothing you could've done," she intervened as if she was inside my head. "But trust me, he'll be back. They always come back. I guess now all you gotta do is decide how long you gone make him wait before taking him back," she said, giving a trivial eye roll.

"Are you crazy? The man slept with my sister. He has not a chance in hell."

"Listen," she said, smacking her lips. "A man gone be a man; you just gotta figure out which one is the one you think is worth the hurt. They all cheat, they all lie, and they all…"

"Hit?"

She took a long pause before she cut her eyes at me. "I don't know what you're talking about."

"So, tell me this, Desiree… how long your man been goin' upside your head? I guess enough times that you feel you deserve to be hurt, huh?" I retorted, answering my own question.

Desiree leaped from the bed, noticeably agitated.

"Listen, I ain't one to judge, and being that I don't even know you, I'd prefer that we keep it that way. I don't take too kindly to uppity bitches that walk around with their noses in the air like they shit smell like roses."

"I didn't mean…"

"Save it," she replied, cutting me off with her hand.

"Like I said, I'm only doing this for C.J., so you can stay in Lala land as long as you need to. My shift is about to end, and…"

"I didn't mean anything by it. I just know where you are, you know? I have been there," I whispered painfully.

Desiree smacked her lips for a second time. "Like I said, I don't know what the hell you're talking about. I don't know where you been, but I'm good over here."

I sat in silence, regretting even opening my big mouth in the first place. Desiree walked over and sat beside me, placing her hand on mines.

"You know why my mom named me Love?" I asked, staring into space as a tear fell down my cheek. "Well, aside from me being born on Valentine's day and all." I chuckled. "She said, nobody ever gets tired of loving; they don't get tired of love. They just get tired of waiting, apologizing, getting disappointed, and being hurt. But in the end, everyone longs for, yearns and most of all loves love."

4

Now is Not the Time

MY DADDY ALWAYS TOLD me that women are like accessories; you use them for what they are suitable for and then rotate 'em out. If all I knew about how to treat a woman was based on what I learned from my pops, then I'd be one hell of a brotha. When I left my father's house, I didn't plan on taking anything with me, not even his long-life lessons that he forced upon me day in and day out. I wanted no parts of him, not even his name, which is why I prefer C.J. over Chris any day. I stood over my father's grave at the crack of dawn, unmoved that there had been a wedge so far between us that I still have yet to shed a tear over his death.

I wandered in silence across the dirt, stopping at the most recent to date that read:

In Loving Memory of
Neveah Marie Nelson
09-08-12 - 07-04-16

I rubbed my fingers across the head stone remorsefully. "I wish I could lay down all my burdens, baby girl. I gotta make it right. I need to make this right," I whispered, holding back my tears.

My blood began to boil as I pictured the beautiful soul that rested beneath my feet due to a disaster in which she did not deserve. Every time I stepped foot on a gravesite, darkness clouds over me, reminding me that as many people I have put in the grave, it's only a matter of time in which I must face my own mortality; but after last night, I realized that now is not that time.

The Night Prior…

I raised my gun slowly, and eventually, the cold tip of the barrel kissed my temple. I closed my eyes as my trigger finger curled naturally….

"Father, forgive me," I whispered.

The sound of a loud bang startled me, along with the commotion that followed. I shuffled across the room and peered out of the blinds to get a better understanding of what was taking place outside of my co-worker's empty house. He would let me come here from time to time to clear my head, at least until he found a buyer. I chuckled as I watched the woman on the passenger side pull her pants up hurriedly. My eyes shifted rapidly as I scanned the scene. I watched in entertainment as the woman in the black Honda shot daggers in the direction of the Silver Durango. She retrieved a black .22 out of the glove box and shoved it into her bag.

"Dammit," I spat as I threw on my grey sweats and Nike slides and darted out the door.

I had made it through the crowd just in time as I gripped her wrist forcefully. "You don't wanna do this, ma. He ain't worth it," I whispered calmly.

After all the commotion and a little convincing, I was able to get the lady into my ride, park hers and assure her that I would get her somewhere to clear her head for the night; hell, it was either that or jail.

"This betta be good, Chris," my brother snapped, answering the phone.

"Aye, I need to come by your spot real fast. I got a lady friend that I need to crash over there for a sec," I countered as I wrapped my shirt around the lady's forearm.

There was a long pause, followed by smacking and slurping noises.

"Damn, do you come up fa air? Let me take this call…shit…whoooo…"

"Tae!" I screamed in agitation.

"Damn bro, you can't come here. I'm a lil busy; go to the Hampton and tell Desi to let you."

I rubbed my temples in disbelief, "Bro, tell me you ain't got another woman in your house?"

He sighed in annoyance. "Desi at work. She doesn't get off for a few hours, C.J. Just take her there and..."

I hung up the phone in disgust and put my car in drive.

"What's your name?" I asked, shifting my eyes between her and the road.

Her head rested against the window like she was in her own zone, so I decided to leave her there. I turned up my radio and let some good Neo Soul play through the speakers. Vivian Greens voice sang, "last night I cried tossed and turned," to the lady's soul, sending a stream of tears down her cheeks. Her hands came up and wiped them away; she closed her eyes and inhaled shakily.

I couldn't resist watching her in curiosity. I wondered her ethnicity; she had an exotic look to her. Her black eyebrows dominated her round face and her natural curls rested wildly against her honey skin, even as she slept. Her full lips poked out as she folded her arms across her chest. Although I could see the hurt on her face, she had an angelic look to her as she slept. I could feel the tremors running through her body. I drove in silence and wondered how much she had endured, how many times had her heart been broken, and how broken she actually was. While these are things that crossed my mind, I had no intentions of letting my mind take me any further than that thought, that's for damn sure.

. . .

We hadn't stepped a foot into the suite before she darted into the restroom and curled into the corner. Before I could go after her, Desi grabbed me gently, stopping me in my tracks.

"Give her some time. If what you told me was true, she's gon' be in a world of her own for a little while," she said, staring through the lady.

"So, how did the party go last night?" She questioned, catching me off guard.

"Huh? Oh, yea, it was cool," I lied.

She chuckled mockingly, "You always gotta be the hero, saving hoes and shit."

"Why she gotta be a hoe, Des?" I countered.

She frowned at me and pursed her lips. "Not her, Chris. Your brother."

"Des, check it, over the years, I've grown to love you like my own sister. The sister that I never had," I assured her. "But I don't like being pulled...."

"I know, Chris," Desiree said, waving her hand dismissively. "It's just... I don't get it; y'all are like night and day. He is nothing like you, that's for sure."

"That's for damn sure." I chuckled cockily as I stroked my chin. "There ain't another me. I'm one of a kind woman," I said, pulling her in for a sincere hug.

Gone Already

I **DIDN'T WANT TO** go home; I couldn't face the man that my husband had become. Many times, I envisioned jumping into my vehicle and leaving without a trace.

"If you even think about leaving me, you best believe I will find you." Dontae's words replayed in my head, dismissing any thoughts I ever had of starting over.

He wasn't like this in the beginning, or was he? Either way, I was tired, tired of the drama, the baby mamas, the late nights, and the fights.

"The fights." I thought to myself as I ran my finger over the bruise beneath my eye. Dontae putting his hands on me was all the reason why I picked up the graveyard shift. I figured the later I worked, the more likely he'd be sleeping like a baby when I got off. Sometimes it worked and others....

I pulled into my driveway, thanking God that all the lights in the house were out, especially since I got off a whole hour early. I took a deep breath, grabbed my bag, and prepared myself for the unexpected. I walked up to my driveway and noticed a manila envelope on the windshield of Tae's black Lambo. I raised my eyebrows and grabbed the envelope, eager to see what was inside. Something told me deep down in my soul that I didn't want to know, so I stuffed it inside my bag, making a mental note to check it once I was settled.

Once I entered the home, I sat my things on the sofa and enabled the alarm system. My eyebrows furrowed as I could

9

hear the music playing from our bedroom. My knees buckled as my blood pressure shot up instantly; it felt like the bones inside of my legs were going to break with every step I took. As I got closer to my bedroom, I could hear Trey Songs serenading the whole damn atmosphere. My heart was beating so hard, I wouldn't be surprised if the neighborhood heard it. I put my hand on the door knob and turned it slowly, pushing the door open. I could see the roses on the bedroom floor; the candles blazed, setting a path to the master bathroom.

Before I could grab his walking stick, Dontae appeared in the door frame; his 6'2, chocolate, athletic stature glistened as the towel was wrapped around his lower region.

"What's up, baby? Did you miss me?" He asked, with a cunning smirk on his face, exposing his deep dimples.

My husband was so handsome that no matter what, whenever I would see him, my feelings would reset, and I would fall in love all over again. No matter how tired I was, I guess I was never tired enough to walk away.

After a warm well-needed bubble bath, a back massage, and some good loving, I laid restlessly underneath my husband's arm, stroking the side of his face as he slept in peace. Lord only knows how bad I wanted to slap him so hard that his slob would create a river larger than Mississippi's most refined just so he could see how the shit felt for a change.

"What happened to you?" I whispered as I kissed his forehead.

Dontae frightened me as he adjusted himself. He wrapped his arms around me as he snuggled against me, resting his head in my bosom.

"Life happened, baby. Life got the best of me. But I'm gone make it right, Desi. I promise," He answered groggily, catching me off guard.

Though his words were like a broken record, the same ole sorry on repeat, my heart ached for him. I felt his pain, hurt and wanted to make everything that he had ever endured disappear. If only it were that simple. I know people would never understand how one could want to take away the pain from a person that seemed set on bringing nothing but pain to them. Sometimes I don't even know why I felt the need to stay and be his punching bag, and maybe I never will. But one thing's for sure, my vows mean everything to me. I'm just waiting on the better that somehow got lost in the worse.

I sat at the edge of my white Italian leather sofa, drinking a glass of cognac. With every sip I took, the more numb I'd become to the burning sensation. The tears trickled down my face uncontrollably. A mixture of waterworks and snot filled my face, but that was the least of my concern. I gave up everything for Dontae; the drama with him is getting old and worn out. If it isn't one thing, it's another. I shook my head in disgust, thinking about how I let myself get to this point. How things had spun so far out of control was beyond me.

I met Dontae at a photoshoot for Sports Illustrated. I was one of the hottest, most requested models coming out of Chicago, and at 18 years old, I was going places. Dontae was a combination of charming, handsome, and, let's not forget, paid. Every time he had a shoot in the Chi, he demanded me and only me. Being that he was one of the highest-paid Quarterbacks in history, he could afford whatever price I spit out. After a year of us dating, he decided that no woman of his, needed to work and damn sure didn't need to be plastered over magazines for other men to admire. At first, I thought that shit was cute, but that wore off over the years; 10 years, to be exact. A little over a year ago, after he got injured in the super bowl, I convinced him to let me work at the hotel to help out my aunt. Being that she was over a few franchises, she needed someone reliable and trustworthy to oversee the one in the city.

"Why are you sitting in the dark, Desi?" Came the voice of Dontae as he flicked on the lights. He strolled over to me

11

and stood over my small frame. "What's wrong now?" He sighed, leaning in for a kiss.

I turned my head, stiffening under his touch. I snatched the papers from the sofa and rose up before him. My voice was strangled, as were my insides.

"What's this Dontae?" I asked, waving the papers in the air. "How could you, Tae?" I grilled, giving him no room to answer. "After all we have been through! The many times I've turned my head to these other bitches and your antics. Don't even try to lie because I know more than you give me credit for," I confirmed, gritting my teeth. "But you couldn't even respect me enough to be careful?" I screamed, painfully shoving the papers into his chest.

Confusion filled his face as he scanned the pictures, "You pregnant?"

I wiped my tears with my arms, poking my chest out, sniffling in between breaths, "No, not me," I countered, brushing past him and up the stairs.

"Whoa, baby...wait...what?"

"It was on your car, Tae."

"So... and what that mean, Desi?"

I stopped and turned to face him; the rage in my eyes scorching through him.

"Nothing. Besides the fact that there was a note attached with your name on it." I argued, grabbing my suitcase.

"Where the hell you think you goin'?" He snapped, grabbing my arm so tight, I could feel the veins crying for freedom

"I can't do this no more, I..."

Slap

The force from his hand sent me flying across the room. I slid back into the corner, pulling my knees into my chest. My eyes shifted, following him as he paced the floor, mumbling

12

his weak-ass apologies and how I made him do it. He was so busy in his zone playing the blame game, he didn't even see me slither out the room. I ran down the stairs, skipping steps as my heart raced. I just needed to make it to the door. I grabbed my purse from the sofa, jetted out, hopped in my ride, and peeled out of the driveway.

"Desiiiiiiiiiiiiii!" He bellowed. But it was too late. I was gone already!

Dontae

Poppa was a Rolling Stone

I BANGED THE STEERING wheel in frustration as I drove like a bat out of hell down Lake Shore Drive. I wrecked my brain, trying to contemplate where she could've gone. I made her cut off all her hating-ass friends years ago. All her family was out south and...

"Chris," I whispered in relief, knowing that whenever shit hit the fan, Desi always called on C.J. to clear her head. I retrieved my phone from the console and called his phone back to back, pissed that he kept sending me to voicemail. I pressed my feet on the brakes and took the Wacker exit, headed west towards his spot.

Pulling up to my brother's house, I sat in the car to have a brief recap of my life. I thought about my brother. He and I were eight months apart. It doesn't take a rocket scientist to realize we ain't come from the same womb. C.J. was born with a silver spoon in his mouth, raised in the suburbs, white picket fences, butlers, went to Harvard University; y'all get my drift. See, all that shit didn't make me no difference. I grew up in the projects, mama on food stamps, standing on the street corners, so I could be the man for my family that our father refused to be. Chris had a white mother, rest her soul, and though we were blood brothers, half of him already came with privilege; at least that's how I saw it. As for me, I was the spitting image of my pops, and I couldn't even get his name. Ain't that some shit? I leaned back in my seat, trying to figure out how I had even become an epitome of the man that I barely even knew. Look at that. He tried to keep me from inheriting anything that

14

was attached to him, and I became everything he was and more.

I stared into the bleachers, wishing he would appear out of nowhere with a sign that had my name on it. I would take my team to the states, and he would be there cheering me on, saying, "That's my boy," with a look of satisfaction. I had wished that every game since I started playing up until my senior year of high school. But the only one that ever showed up for me was my grandmother; no matter what, she was at every game screaming, "that's my baby, I raised him, make Nana proud, baby!" With tears of joy in her eyes. After my mother lost her job at the College for some bullshit allegations from one of the seniors, she had gotten lost in her own world, and my Nana Gene was always there to pick up her pieces.

"Baby, I know it's been hard for you, and I want you to know how proud of you I am, and I have always been," My nana said, removing my helmet from my head as I knelt before her.

"I know ya Mama ain't always been able to give you the best childhood." Her lips quivered as she fought back the tears. I opened my mouth to console her, but she put her finger over my lips. "Just listen, baby. No matter how hard this road has been, I wouldn't change my path, take any shortcuts, or even a sharp right if I could. You were worth it all," she said as she cleared her throat in an attempt to slow the cascade that was itching to fall from her eyes. "Now go out there and kick some ass and make yo Nana proud!" She smiled, shoving my helmet into my chest.

I rose up, placing my helmet underneath my armpit. I grabbed her hands and brought them to my lips.

"Not only am I going to make you proud, but I'm also gone make you rich and get us out the hood," I promised, kissing her hands.

"Dontae, you're in!" My coach shouted.

I ran off as my grandmother watched me in bliss, keeping my promise and never turning back.

"How long she been gone, Tae?" C. J asked, bringing me a glass of Martel.

"About an hour," I answered, rubbing my temples. "What the hell was I thinking?" I asked myself aloud.

"Yea, bro. Tell me…what were you thinking?"

"I should have knocked her ass out. Bet she wouldn't have got away then, now would she?"

"Are you serious?" Chris asked me in disbelief. My jaw twitched at the very thought that he would think I was playing.

"Do it look like I'm playing?" I answered as I raised my brow looking him firmly in his eyes. I picked up my phone and called Desi for the hundredth time.

Chris stroked his chin, contemplating taking this conversation to another level. I'm guessing that he ain't want these problems by the look on my face, not today. I wasn't in the mood for teaching, preaching, or none of that shit.

"You got sixty seconds," Desiree answered dryly. I hopped up in surprise. My eyes widened at the sound of her voice.

"Where you at, baby?" I asked sincerely. We need to talk…I'm so…."

"Dontae, I'm not trying to hear that shit! You wanna talk? Go talk to the woman that's carrying your baby."

"I don't even know if it's my baby; it could be anybody's baby. That girl…." The silence on the other end let me know I had messed up. Losing my patience, I gritted my teeth and did the one thing I did best. "You got twenty-four hours to make your way home, or I'm gone make yo life a living hell. I already told you, till death do us part, and I meant that shit!" I threatened, hanging up the phone.

C.J. looked at me in disgust, but I ain't give a damn. We stared at one another in annoyance. Deep down inside, I hated this joker. We had the same blood, but we ain't fight the same fight. He was nothing like me; he was nothing like my father, and here he was, left to carry my father's name and legacy. I tossed my glass back and finished my drink, then brushed past him and out the door. Chris didn't deserve to live under the same roof as my pops. Was I mad at my father for being who he was? Hell naw! There is always another side to the story, and I held on to the hope that his version was all the confirmation I needed. I didn't need to live under his roof for the apple not to fall far from the tree. I got it, honestly. Poppa was a rolling stone, and so was his firstborn.

Love

Cry Me a River

WHEN THE RAYS OF daybreak snuck through the drapes, I was beyond worn out. I hadn't slept one bit, and my bloodshot eyes singed from exhaustion. I forced myself out of the king-sized bed and powered back on my cell. I shook my head in disgust as it began to go crazy in my hand, showing the missed texts and calls. Jamel and my half-sister, Raelyn, had called repeatedly. Every time I'd pictured them two together in the truck that I purchased, might I add, my heart broke a little more.

My emotions alternated between fits of rage and uselessness. Notions of retaliation ran through my head as I lay in the darkness of the room. I hadn't slept in days, and my appetite just didn't exist. I scrolled through my phone, and there was one name that gave me a glimmer of grace. I smiled tenderly and returned the call to the one person that I knew would go to war for and with me with no questions asked.

"Love! You and I are gone fight. I've been blowing you up for the past three days like we are in a committed relationship or some shit. On top of that, I went by your place, and the driver window of the truck was broken, glass all on the seats. Jamel answered the door and said, you went crazy, and he hasn't heard from you in a week. I was two steps away from laying his ass out, thinking he done went O.J. on yo ass, and I couldn't have that. What is going on? Alexis hasn't heard from

18

you; Raelyn was standing at the door looking all…. wait… what the hell was Raelyn doing there anyway?"

"I need you to come to get me, Sage," I whispered groggily, trying to fight back every tear I had left in me.

"Love? What's wrong? Whose ass do I need to kick…"

I closed my eyes, trying to fight the burning sensation of the tears struggling emission.

"I'll tell you everything when you get here. I'm downtown at the Hampton. I just need…"

The phone clicked, and I already knew Sage was on her way.

You didn't come across too many friendships like myself, Alexis, and Sage. We were the three musketeers, and each of us served a particular purpose in one another's lives. Sage and I are one and the same in most ways, so she was more my echo or a sounding board of some sort. Where Alexis is a lot younger, but she's wise and street smart. She tells me what I need; she doesn't sugarcoat a damn thing; she gives it to me straight up and in the raw. Although I ain't have time for nobody patting me on the back trying to tell me how we can turn lemons into lemonade, I needed someone, some comfort, and some positive vibes; I required some Sage.

I could feel myself losing it, and I didn't know what to do. It hadn't been a whole week since things went down, and I was already breaking under the pressure of it all. After all, sometimes, the temporary sanity I would receive by forgiving Jamel seemed so much better than the ongoing hurt of walking away and starting over. And at this moment in time, I wanted this pain to end now.

TY NESHA

My fingers trembled as I held the phone to my ear. I sat and listened to all 10 voicemails and read 12 text messages of, *"baby, come home, and I'm sorry."* I was so damn tired of hearing that *"I'm sorry"* shit, especially coming from a sorry muthafucka that only felt remorse for one thing; getting caught.

When Jo, played by Janet Jackson in that *For Colored Girls* movie, said, "Save your sorry. One thing I don't need is anymore apologies. I got sorry greeting me at the front door. You can keep yours." I felt that in my bones.

The phone vibrated in my hand, startling me. I dropped the phone on the mattress unconsciously, wincing at the thought of having a cracked screen.

"Baby? Love? You there, baby?" Jamel's voice came through the other end of the phone, catching me off guard.

"Shit," I hissed as I picked the phone back up and put it to my ear.

"Why do you keep calling my phone, Jamel?" I said sternly.

I don't care how hard I cried; one thing I had to learn was to never let a man see how messed up he had you. I swallowed hard and prayed that through this call, I would be strong enough to...

"Listen baby."

"Baby? Negro, you really got some nerve."

"Can I please talk, Love? See...that there is our problem now; you always gotta have the last say. You can't never let me be the man."

Amused and disgusted, I took the phone off my ear and looked at it like it was gone to say the wrong number or something.

"Let you? You tell me this... how can a woman let a man be a man? Last I checked, you don't need permission to do what it is you're more than capable of. And don't you dare try

20

to switch this around on me! If you had a problem with me, or us, should I say, that doesn't create an automatic pass to screw my sister or any bitch for that matter. Take accountability, fool." I hissed, feeling the tremors in my voice.

"You right, baby. I messed up, and I swear I'm going to make it up to you. We better than anything that tries to break us, baby."

I sighed deeply, trying to shake the images of him and my sister in that truck from my head.

I closed my eyes and felt a lone tear make its way down my cheek. It was all going so well between him and me. Raelyn hadn't even been staying with us a whole week before she stabbed me in my back yet again. It was like every time I think I'm getting somewhere, reach a point in which I can rebuild, smile, and be happy, something crazy comes along and infiltrates my life. I wanted to forgive this man. I want to believe that he had messed up, and we would try again; get married, be happy, and make it work; it started to dawn on me that it never would.

I took a deep breath and exhaled sharply, "You are right, Jamel. You messed up, you broke us; boo hoo hoo cry me a river, nigga. And when you're done, jump in that muthafucka," I countered before I ended our call and added him to my block list immediately.

I turned on my Pandora and let K Michelle's radio play through my cell phone. Whenever I got tired of a man, she was always my 'go-to.' It was like she was singing me her own little lullaby.

I stepped into the shower and inhaled the steam, allowing it to clear up any stuffiness the tears and sobs had created. The hot water dispensed over me as I sang every word, wishing my phone would crank up louder.

"Cause if I let him do it, I did it to myself
And I was so dumb, I need it, I need some help!

21

TY NESHA

'Cause all that I can see is that she is prettier than me
Damn, I wish I had her body! I can hear my self-esteem
I don't like me, me, Me!

Soul Sisters

B Y THE TIME I arrived at the hotel, I had spotted my
friend standing at the curbside. I pulled up and watched
her as she had no idea I was sitting right in front of her.
Her naturally arched eyebrows furrowed as if she were in deep
thought. A little over a year ago, she had begun to have
episodes in which she would zone out and go into another
world, not even remembering where she was. She had found a
way to escape reality which had become a coping mechanism
for her. Love's curly copper hair was pulled back from her
round angelic face, exposing her big brown eyes that stared
into space. Her oversized coral, My Black, *is Beautiful* shirt hung
off her shoulders, contrasting effortlessly against her sun-
kissed skin.

I stepped out of my car, walked to the other side, and
slowly sat beside her, placing my hand on her lap. Sometimes
it would take hours for her to come back to earth, and others,
all it took was a simple touch. She stood to her feet as if she
was in a daze and walked to my car without uttering a single
word.

Love never looked at me as she got into the car. I watched
the tears flow from her eyes as she sniffled in between words.
By the time she had finished telling me what happened, she
was crying so hard that she could barely gather up the strength
to continue. I shook my head empathetically. When she hurts,
I hurt; that shit went both ways. To see my sister hurt cut me

deep. Deep enough to body this fool and her trashy ass sister. I never liked Raelyn's ass. She was sneaky and a two-timing hoe.

That's the thing about so-called "family." They will turn on you quicker than an enemy.

Love and I didn't have to be blood to consider ourselves sisters. She was my blood regardless. I had wiped so many of her tears as she has mines. We both have cried on one another's shoulder many times before, but the profound, gut-wrenching way that her sobs left her told me that this was different. It wasn't just about Love catching Mel cheating; in fact, she had been through many tough times in her life. The letdowns and disloyalty she was equipped to. She was probably one of the toughest and strongest women I had ever met aside from my mother. If life happened to anyone, it happened to Love. Just when she thought she had caught a break, just when she thought she had finally hit a positive turning point in her life, she gets hit with yet another twist.

. . .

The unyielding buzz from my cell phone stirred Love entirely out of her sleep. I hadn't even realized how long I'd been driving; she had been sleeping for about an hour.

"What time is it?" She asked groggily.

I reached for my phone and ignored the call. "3:30," I replied before shooting Alexis a quick text.

I couldn't even press the send button before she bussed through my line again.

"I'm outside," I answered as I pulled up outside of the address she had given me.

"No! Fuck you, you small dick muthafucka. You and yo manly-looking ass mama can go straight to hell!"

My eyes bucked as I put my finger over my lips, signaling for Love not to say anything as I put the call on speaker. Lexi always had some juicy drama going on, and with her mess,

24

there was never a dull moment. When she decided to take it there, nobody was safe. Not ya mama, not ya....

"And yo' bald-headed ass daughter need some Head and Shoulders for her flaky ass scalp too, walking around the house getting dandruff all over my brand-new Coach bag."

Kids. She ain't give a damn who it was. I shook my head and slapped Love across her arm for laughing so hard, trying not to laugh myself.

"Alexis!" I called out, trying to keep my composure.

She came busting out the front door in a frenzy. "Bout time you got here. I was about to go haywire and send the whole South Side up," she said, waving her phone in the air like it was a gun and she was gone set it off.

"Send up that fake ass, Coach Bag," the tall dude following behind her shot back.

Lexis stopped in her tracks, doing a 360 spin. "You got some nerves, Toni, tryna stunt out here in front of the whole neighborhood with that fake ass lining you got upside yo head. Like we can't tell you over here rockin' a Beijing goatee. Keep playing wit' me if you want to. I'll throw this whole cup of Cîroc in yo' face and have you looking like you, a thirteen-year-old boy ducking puberty."

The whole block was laughing so hard; all the dude could do was stare her down. He mugged Lexi so hard, I could feel judgment day approaching. Alexis ain't have no shame either. She tossed back the cup in her hand, finishing up her drink. She wiped her mouth, giving him an evil glare before she hopped in my truck. She rolled down the window, tossed the cup out, and gave him the middle finger before I skirted off.

I looked at her in my rearview as she huffed and puffed, fuming and noticeably irritated. I could see it in her eyes; she was about to start some more mess. Before I could mediate, she dove in headfirst, placing her hand on Love's shoulder.

25

"Word is…"

"Don't you start with me, Alexis." The laughter in Love's face turnt to rage instantly as she gripped Lexi's hand firmly.

I don't know how Lexi always got the gossip before it even hit the streets, but she was the queen of tea.

Love sat up, adjusting herself, now tapping Lexi's hand condescendingly. "Word is, I caught Jamel's cheating behind banging Raelyn in that truck I helped him buy. The same truck you told me not to get. I don't need no…"

I could see Alexis's eyes turn cold. "I told yo ass these men ain't shit. Yea, I said it; Love. I told you so. They all the same! Niggaz cheat on good women with a bird that wears a chain from the beauty supply store that says "bossy." That's why I ain't checkin' for or lookin for a man. I control this." She rolled her eyes, pulling her travel-sized bottle of Cîroc out of her purse, and tossed it back. "And that's why I play they behinds before they can even have me out here…"

"Lexi, shut the hell up! Damn!" I snapped, pulling my car into the hair salon.

I put the car in park and took a deep breath before I turned to face Love. I grabbed her face and turned it towards me slowly. "You don't have to talk, Lovey. Just listen," I said calmly as I gave Lexi a side-eye. She hunched her shoulders nonchalantly, taking another shot.

The aura in the air had changed, and the look on my friend's face worried me. I took a long pause and swallowed. There was so much uneasiness in the air that I felt a palpable heat coming from her. Tensions were high, and it was clear that Love was not in her right mind.

"I need for you to cry as hard as you want to for as long as you need to."

Lexi threw her hands in the air and fell back in the seat dramatically. I rolled my eyes and continued.

"I need you to know that you did nothing wrong, baby girl." I grabbed her hands and bowed my head.

"Dear Heavenly Father, I need you to give my friend strength right now. She has endured so much that I ask you to help calm her soul. Lord, I need you to forgive us in advance; need be, we have to commit some crimes and takes some lives. Yes, Dear Lord, be the light in this time of darkness…"

Love snatched her hand from mines and leaned over to the side.

I raised my eyebrow and smacked my lips. "What's wrong with you? I figured we could pay him a visit and get in and out, if you know what I mean. You know Alexis and me always down for making a mess and being a negro's Karma, no doubt."

Alexis shook her head in confirmation, giving me a high five.

"Sage," Love whispered, looking straight ahead.

"Love? What's wrong, boo?" I asked.

"I need you to do me a huge favor," she said.

"Yea…"

"Move your body five inches to the right. I'm just tryna steer clear from the lightning that is about to strike yo ass in five…four…."

We all laughed briefly, bringing in well-needed energy.

"Check it out!" Lexi said excitedly, pulling out her phone. "There is an event tonight at that new spot across from The House of Blues. That white boy, Sam Smith, is gone be there and…"

"Sam who?" I asked in confusion.

"He's a singer, I guess," Alexis replied, waving her hands dismissively.

"He got a lot of music I can rock with. Pretty slept on if you ask me," Love said, bobbing her head to the beat that only she could hear.

"Yea, him! Anywho, I got three V.I.P. tickets. Y'all in or naw?"

We all looked at one another and agreed in unison. It had been a long time since we had stepped out, and tonight, Chicago was not ready for us to hit the scene.

I looked at my girls and shook my head in amazement at how strong a bond we had formed within a few years. We are not the typical "girl, let me tell you" type of friends that you come across these days. Nowadays, these chicks believe that gossiping and digging for information was what a friendship was about. We were above and beyond that. We were sisters, soul sisters, and nothing could change that, or so we thought.

My Sister's Keeper

I WALKED UP TO the door, and before I could knock, Jamel jerked the door open.

"K...K...Kane? When you get in town?" He asked, stumbling over his words.

The look on his face told me something wasn't right, and I damn sure wasn't liking the fact that he didn't even have the decency to ask me if I wanted to come in.

"Where is my sister?" I asked firmly.

"I don't know, Kane. I ain't seen her in..."

"What you mean you 'ain't' seen her, Mel?" I asked, trying to keep my cool. Something was up. It had been a week since I'd heard from my baby sister. I slid by her place, and her fiancé dared to act like he hadn't seen her either.

"Listen, I messed up," he stated thoughtfully, stepping onto the front porch, pulling the door closed behind him.

I folded my arms as my nose flared. I was ready to crack his head open just off the strength of him not knowing her whereabouts. I made it very clear that I didn't want him messing around with my sister. I also made it clear that if he'd even thought about fucking her over, I would stomp a mudhole in his ass. This is probably the reason my sister never told me anything about their relationship.

I looked him up and down and sucked my teeth in frustration. "Look, this ain't Dr. Phil, and I'm not yo' therapist. So, if this lil mess up is not going to put me in a place of where my sister is, there really isn't anything to discuss."

He plopped down on the front steps and buried his head into his hands. "She left me," he said, shaking his head back and forth.

"Baby, what's goin' on?" A familiar voice spoke from inside the house. Jamel froze in time as my jaw began to flinch overpoweringly. He tried to stop me by grabbing my leg. I damn near kicked his teeth out, shaking him off and pushing through the door.

"Kane…Wait…" Before she could finish, I yoked her up, gripping my hands around her neck and slamming her against the wall.

"I always knew you were trifling, Raelyn, but you would do this shit to yo' own blood? Over some…"

Her eyes were so wide, I didn't even realize how tight my grip was around her neck. Releasing my grasp, I could feel the blood inside of my body boiling so hot, my touch alone would give somebody a third-degree burn.

"I'm sorry," she sobbed, gasping for air as she fell limp to the floor, rubbing the fingerprints around her neck.

I looked past her and noticed Jamel standing in the doorway like a weak ass bum. I charged towards him in rage as he attempted to stop me, holding his hand into space. I punched him so hard, I could hear the bones in his jaw crack. That didn't prevent me from connecting another to his right jaw, sending him tumbling down the stairs. I skipped down the stairs and pulled my shirt over my head.

"Get up pussy!" I demanded through clenched teeth, putting my hands up.

Jamel staggered side to side before regaining his balance. I inched closer toward him, sending a quick left hook to his fractured jaw.

"Aargh!" He groaned, buckling to his knees in pain before hitting the ground.

I straddled over him, shoving my fists into his swollen face, knocking blood from his mouth. A look of fear was embedded in his pupils as he shook his head from side to side. Raelyn's screams from behind fueled me more, sending me into a more bottomless rage. If I can't put a whooping on her, he was gone take a beating for the both of 'em. I continued to land hits to his face, head, and body relentlessly until I was out of breath. I stood up and grabbed his arms, pulling him to his feet. We both sweated profusely, trying to catch our breath.

I held him by the collar of his shirt to keep him steady as I leaned into him. "This ass-whooping has been a long time coming," I said as I flattened his collar and tapped him lightly on his chest. "Now go clean yo' self-up and start packing."

"Packing?" He blew in confusion.

I gripped my door handle and stopped in my tracks. I took a deep breath, not allowing my emotions to show. I spoke slowly and collected, so there wouldn't be any misunderstandings. "I don't care who you are or how long you think we have been cool. I have, and I always will be my sister's keeper. I will die for mines. Don't you ever forget that. You and that rat better be gone before I get back, or I'm gone make you remember why they used to call me Hurricane."

I dipped in and out of traffic, trying to make it back to my spot. I really didn't know who I was more pissed at, Jamel's sorry ass or myself. I didn't know how in the hell I was

31

supposed to tell my sister that there was a lawsuit against Wrights Realty that could cause us to go bankrupt. My phone ringing took me out of thought.

"What it do?"

"Kane, there's been a change."

"Ok, bet. When and where?" I asked, turning onto a side street.

"I'll hit you with a date and location in a few," he added.

"Cool." I agreed before ending the call.

I scrunched my face in annoyance. I hated being left in the dark, but I knew I needed this deal to fall through, and I had to do what was required by any means necessary. I had a plan. A plan that could take the agency to the top, legally. It took all I had not to turn back to my old ways. I hadn't figured out how to balance life here in the corporate world. I had the whit, the hustle, and the mindset, but something about the street life fascinated me. Hustling was all I ever knew. I ain't never been one to stick my hand out and ask nobody for nothing. Just like I had never asked my grandfather to hand me Wrights Realty. Here I was, just getting out of a five-year bid, ready to take my squad to a whole new level, and I get a call that threw a wrench in my entire orchestration.

"What the hell is this?" I asked, pushing the papers back to the attorney that sat across from me.

"Your grandfather left you his real estate agency. He wanted no one to carry the family business besides his first and only grandson."

I laughed sarcastically. "Hell no! I don't know the first thing about real estate."

Love leaned in, whispering in my ear, "I thought you said you took a real estate class while you were locked down. With that and the trade you have in architecture, you can do it, Kane. This is your second chance."

"No, I can't, Love."

The earsplitting sound of the horns and screeching tires brought me out of my thoughts. I sat at the light in disbelief. The delirious woman staggered through traffic, swerving cars confusedly. I put my car in park and exited my vehicle to get to the lady. Before I could wrap my head around what was happening, I froze in time as she leaped in front of the semi-truck recklessly.

Hell on Earth

THE MUTED SYMPHONY OF beeping monitors and pinging elevators startled me. I stared into the ceiling in confusion. My eyes shifted swiftly around the room; the immense pain in my head made it difficult for me to turn. I remained still, yet the quiet droning in the hospital corridors was replaced by an unfamiliar voice.

"You gone tell me why you thought it was wise to step in front of that big ass truck?" He asked in a hushed tone.

My eyes remained still. I winced as he leaned in and attempted to place his hand on my shoulder.

"My bad. I wasn't trying to scare you. I was just trying to help. I'm harmless, I swear," he said, leaning back and throwing his hands up.

I watched him out of my peripheral vision as he licked his full lips before standing to his feet. I surveyed his medium stature as he brushed the dirt off his black slacks. I slowly turned my head, and the most beautiful man I had ever laid eyes on stood at my bedside.

"If you are so harmless, why am I lying in the hospital bed with my head wrapped in an ace bandage?" I grunted while patting my head.

"Now that wasn't intentional. I was trying to save yo' ass from being smashed into tomorrow by that truck. I pushed you

34

out the way, and it just so happened to be a brick that broke your fall, and uh, it knocked you unconscious," he concluded, clearing his throat and scratching his head.

"Who in the hell asked for your help?" I hissed, smacking my lips. I was far beyond annoyed at the fact that he wanted to play "Captain Save a Hoe" in the heat of the night.

He chuckled and shook his head, showing a glimpse of his chipped tooth. Usually, I wasn't big on a man with a busted grill, but even that was sexy as hell. I examined him closely. His broad figure put me in the mind of a convicted felon released after a ten-year bid. He was solid and chocolate. His hair was low, but his deep waves gave him a pretty boy look. He stood about 5'11 and 220 easy. The oversized tat on his neck screamed *"gangster,"* but I was still turned on. I took a breath and managed to grimace, trying not to give away any desirability that this man's presence had demanded. His almond-shaped eyes were glued to me, making me uncomfortable.

Feeling nauseous, I sat up and swung my legs around the bed. I tried to hide the pain I was feeling, but my body ached all over. I leaped from my bed as I rushed to the bathroom just in time. I heaved violently, hugging the toilet as I could feel the mixtures of liquor doing a dance inside me, causing my insides to explode.

"That looks painful," the annoying guy stated as he stood in the door frame.

"You think?" I spat sarcastically as I wiped the slob from my mouth with the back of my hand.

"Oh, nah, I ain't talking about that," he said sternly. I turned my head towards him. His eyes were glued to the bruise on my back.

I struggled to my feet and snatched the hospital gown closed. "Do you mind?" I snapped, pushing him out of the way and slamming the door shut.

35

TY NESHA

I stood over the sink to rinse my mouth. My body hurt so bad as I struggled to stand up straight. "Ugh!" I groaned as I used the bathroom counter to pull myself up.

I looked at myself in the mirror. At that moment, I didn't even recognize the woman staring back at me. That woman was a direct reflection of what I felt like: broken, damaged, and drained. I stood there and wondered how much worse things would get. I rubbed my fingers across my swollen lip and thought back to earlier today.

Earlier That Day...

I woke up to the cold feeling of the tiles against my face. My head throbbed as I tried to recall how I ended up lying on the bathroom floor in the first place. It had been almost a week since I had left home, and after running for so long, I realized that I had nowhere else to go. I hadn't even been to work. I had been informed that he had been up there twenty-five times since I'd left. Ignoring the feeling in my gut, I decided to go home against my better judgment.

To say this beating was the worst would be an understatement. I hurt every time I breathed in, taking tiny breaths to ease the pain. My eye was swollen and different shades of black, and blue radiated off my chocolate skin. I cracked open the bathroom door to check my surroundings. Tae was nowhere in sight, so I stepped out. Making sure to be extra quiet, I tip-toed down the hall, slowly walking towards the window; his car was not there. I stared outside my home, shaking my head as the tears flowed down my face.

Realizing what today was, a ray of hope was bestowed upon me. I reckoned he wouldn't be home for a while. Every Friday, Tae would go play Poker and gamble his life away faithfully. He wouldn't return home until Sunday afternoon. This was his routine for the past five years. With that single thought, I was on autopilot.

No sooner than I had stepped down the stairs, my heart sank into my chest as I spotted Dontae sitting at the edge of the couch looking like a madman. He looked like he hadn't shaved in years, and the house reeked of liquor and marijuana. My heart hit the floor. I debated turning around and booking it, but I couldn't move.

36

"Where the hell you think you going, Desiree?" He asked calmly, taking a puff from his blunt.

Again, I was stuck. I opened my mouth to speak, but no words would come out.

"Cat got yo' tongue, Desi?" He asked as he rose from his seat and walked towards me.

We both just stood there in silence. My eyes shifted around the room for something to hit him with, but nothing was in my reach. I flinched as he stuck his hand out and stroked my face. His eyes were so soft at that moment, and in an instant, they changed. He gripped a handful of my hair and yanked my head back, throwing me to the floor. Before I could move, he lifted his leg and brought it down on my back so hard, it felt like he had shifted some organs.

I cried silently because I refused to let him hear me weep or even plead. If he was going to kill me, then so be it. Tonight, I would fight.

Right before he connected another kick, I mustered up enough strength to roll over on my back and kick him dead in his balls with as much force as I could, sending him hurled over. I immediately got up and ran towards the kitchen area; he was right on my heels. I grabbed the knife from the counter just in time to jab it into his gut. His knees buckled to the floor as he held his stomach in more shock than pain. I hadn't seen so much blood in my life as it seeped through his fingers like running water. I leaned over him, now placing pressure on his wound with my left hand. I knelt before him and kissed him on the forehead as he pleaded for me to get help. My eyes filled with tears, and something inside of me turned cold. I knew that as long as I was married to Dontae, I was a dead woman walking. Life with him was hell on earth, and the end was starting to sound inviting. I took the knife and shoved it into his chest. At that moment, everything went black.

When Love Calls

I SLAMMED MY LAPTOP shut in frustration. It seemed like nothing was going according to my plans. And after leaving my doctor, I really wasn't in the mood for the fuckery. I dialed my brother's number for what seemed to be the hundredth time, and just like the last 99, it went straight to voicemail. I sat there and pondered on how the hell I let myself get enfolded up in this bull in the first place. I left the street life in Boston when I left two and a half years ago. How I got mixed back up in this mess is beyond me. Oh yea, I have my new-found brother to thank for that...

Two Years Prior

My brother and my childhood friend, Dominick, stumbled through my office door, staggering side to side; my brother was almost unrecognizable as the blood seeped from his head.

"Tae? What the hell happened, bruh?" I asked, jolting out of my chair.

Dominic, almost half his size, was basically carrying my brother. I rushed over to help him to the chair. My insides were boiling as I tried to hide my rage and remain calm.

I cringed at how much he looked like my father, and after getting to know him over the years, I quickly learned that he had inherited his

38

cunning and womanizing ways as well—all in all, that didn't stop him from being my brother. Though my father had no issue disowning his own flesh and blood, that was a characteristic I didn't inherit.

"I got a call from one of my partners. They responded to a disturbance out south. By the time they got there, Dontae here was lying there beaten to a bloody pulp," Dominic said, pulling me off to the side.

He leaned in, speaking under his breath. "Listen, C.J., the people that did this intended for him to survive. They did this to send a message; more of a warning, so to speak. These cats are big-time Loan Sharks."

"Loan Sharks?" I hissed through clenched teeth. Looking over at my brother.

"What the hell is he..."

"I don't know, C.J., but this shit is out of my pay grade; you feel me? Your brother is in some deep shit with some powerful people, and he gone continue to get this beating on sight unless he either pay the people or..."

The loud factory beat from my phone interrupted my thoughts. I took a deep breath and folded my hands on top of the desk. My eyebrows furrowed as I tried to process how things had all played out.

"Tell me something good, Dominick," I answered tensely.

"You know I could lose my job behind this, right?"

"I know, bruh. I just need to know, man. I haven't slept or ate since it broadcasted all over the news. My mind won't let me rest until I know."

"What if?"

"C'mon man, I don't want you giving me no speech on how sometimes the unknown is best. Not in this case."

There was a long pause before he let out an exasperating breath. "We should have the results back as soon as I can get them out of the system. I must move cautiously with this one.

But I'll get to it as soon as possible. With that, I'll have an answer for you."

"I owe you one, Dom."

"I still think, worst-case scenario, things are not going to play out well if you know. It's been handled. I handled it for you.... just..."

The light taps at the door saved me from a lecture of the year.

"I 'preciate you, Dom. I gotta get back to it," I said as I motioned for Jade, one of the bartenders at my new club, to enter.

Jade walked behind me and poured me a drink. Before I knew it, she kissed me on the shoulder, working her soft lips up to my neck. I knew every bit of this was gone distract me from what I had to do, but I dismissed that from my head instantly. I watched as she sauntered over to the door and twisted the lock. She paused briefly before turning to face me, giving me a seductive glare. My eyes stayed on her as she made her way back towards me.

My manhood throbbed as she massaged it through the fabric of my pants. I gripped her lower region and lifted her onto my desk, slipping my fingers underneath her skirt, allowing them to make their way inside her. She let her head back and moaned softly. The base from the music across the room drowned out Jade's unconstrained moans and groans. I teased her briefly, knowing I wasn't going to be able to finish the mess I was generating, but I enjoyed making her wait impatiently. I let my fingers serenade her insides until her body began to jerk uncontrollably. I smirked arrogantly like a proud man and licked my lips as I watched her beg for mercy.

I adjusted my suit jacket before making my way into the V.I.P. section of my lounge. To ensure everything was all ready to go before we opened those doors, I solidified things myself. I had no time for mess-ups or fragmentary business. I nodded my head in approval as the crowd began to form and the vibe of the music led the way.

Jade stood behind the bar creating revenue as she finessed the customers effortlessly. She smiled at me as I walked in her direction.

"Mr. James, you have someone that would like to speak with you about an act," Jade said from behind the bar as she sat the glass of Louis in front of me.

"The club isn't hiring any new…"

"Hello, Mr.?" A soft voice sang in my ear, taking a seat next to me on a barstool. She turned to face me as she stuck her hand out.

"James…" I replied, grabbing her hand and bringing it to my lips, gracing her with a gentle peck.

"I'm sorry to barge in on you, but tonight, I wanted to see if my friend could be an opening act for…"

"Whoa, whoa, opening act? We don't sign on any new acts the night of," Jade interjected.

"She's right, ma'am," I said nonchalantly.

"Listen, my friend, she will blow this sucka down, and you have my word on it."

"Mr. James doesn't take acts or the chance to jeopardize the reputation of the club based on some '*home girl*' from around the way's word," Jade countered.

I raised my hand to silence her, pissing her off, of course.

"I'm sorry, there is nothing I can do to help you," I countered before downing my drink.

"Jade, be sure to show this lady and her friend or friends?" I asked, raising a brow. She nodded in confirmation. "A few rounds of whatever on me," I ordered, pushing my card in her direction.

The lady picked up the card and examined it momentarily before standing. She pursed her lips together, forcing a smile and dropping the card in her bag.

"It's been a pleasure, Mr. James," she said kindly before walking away.

"Better luck next time," Jade poked snidely.

"Jade," I said firmly, cutting my eyes at her.

Jade was fine as hell; she had the potential to be one of the most gorgeous women on the earth, but that's about it. I stared through Jade, aggravated by her conduct. A woman like Jade could never be my lady. She had no motivation, but she was fueled by someone else's money and power. I kept her around because she could bring in the revenue and work the crowd, but nothing more. She was too damn insecure, and it showed terribly.

The lights in the club dimmed as my host spoke into the mic, welcoming the first act of the night. I chuckled at the fact that the bass in his voice was utterly overkilled.

"When Love Calls, one can't help but to answer. This opening act is one that you won't regret. I need everyone to give a warm welcome to…."

The perplexed look on Jade's face almost coordinated with the cunning smirk on the lady's that had returned. As pissed as I wanted to be, I had to give it to her. Whatever she had done had to be clever. Especially if she was able to pull this off with me, the owner, in the same damn room.

Before I could react, I was adorned by the most angelic version of Michel'le's, *Something in My Heart.*

"Youuuuu took my loveeeee and I'm willing, there's no limit to the love I'm giving.... the love I'm givinggggggggggggggggggg.......ohhhhhhhhhhhhhh,..."

Taken off guard, I spun around in my seat, dying to see the face that was behind this dominating voice. I surveyed this woman, starting from the chain-linked ankle straps on her rainbow-colored heels that sat slightly below the denim ripped jeans that suffocated her thick thighs. My eyes worked their way to the top; this sista was nice. The light illuminated over her reddish-brown hair that flowed over her bronze shoulders. Her ruby red lips captivated me as they made love to the microphone.

I stood to my feet and walked a little closer. Our eyes locked, and... "Well, I'll be damned."

Not Interested

A T THIS TIME, in this moment, no one else existed as I stood on this stage and sang my heart out. As social as I am, I hated getting up in front of people. For what, just so they can judge me and pick me apart? Hell no! But tonight, tonight, my friends swayed me to lay it all out and to allow my craft to become my therapy. *"If not any other time, at least you could tonight."* Lexi's slick behind stated. At first, I was pissed that Alexis had the nerve to put me on the spot tonight. She had a way of doing things that would make you wanna strangle her and hug her afterward. In the end, there was always a method to her madness.

After a standing ovation and two encores, I figured I could put down the mic and enjoy the rest of my evening. The host grabbed my hand and assisted me off the stage, but not before whispering a, "Damn baby, you did that, witcho' fine ass," in my ear. I gave him a friendly smile and thanked him kindly before rolling my eyes in my head.

I made my way to the V.I.P. Section. Lexi stood off to the side, chopping it up with the guy that had been gawking at me the whole time. Something about him was familiar. I just couldn't put my finger on it just yet. Sage did her own little shuffle as she made her way towards me, smiling extra hard, showing all of her pearly whites. I smiled back at her and shook my head while she snapped her fingers, tryna lip sing the hook to her favorite Beyonce song.

"I ain't worried, doin' me tonight

A little sweat ain't never hurt nobody

While y'all standin' on the wall

I'm the one tonight gettin' bodied

Gettin' bodied, gettin' bodied

Gettin' bodied, gettin' bodied

Want my body

Won't you get me bodied

My sister was so damn fine, okay! Her version of melanin was my favorite. I always tell her, *"The sun loved you so much; it kissed you twice."* She rocked a short, honey blonde pixy. Our stylist, Co-Co, slayed her pin curls to the hair gawds, baby.

I met Sage a few years ago at a support group for mothers that were considering giving their child up for adoption. She saw something in me that I didn't see in myself. She promised that whatever I decided, she would support me every step of the way, and here we are. Sage was as chill and as laid back as they came. She never did too much, and though she was a "Plain Jane," everything she did stood out naturally. Sage's multi-colored, haltered backless jumpsuit hugged her body to perfection. Her body was banging! One would never even guess she ate the way she did, never gaining a single pound. I lowkey hated her ass for that. Here I was, trying to get it together, and soon as I would even think about eating a fry, ten pounds somehow miraculously appears.

"Oh, my goodness, Love! You kilt it, baby! I'm so proud of you," Sage chirped, pulling me in for a hug.

"Girl, I'm gone kill you hoes in the morning, watch," I said, giving her a slight smirk.

We strolled to our tables, pulled up a seat, and I instantly tossed back two shots, one behind the next.

"Damn girl, slow down," Alexis teased, pulling up a chair next to us.

Before I could clap-back, the waitress sat another round on our table, giving off a vibe that I wasn't feeling at the moment. She and Lexi locked eyes briefly. I nudged Sage, but she was already on board. Lexi pressed her lips together and leaned back, crossing her legs with this cynical grin on her face. We all knew that things wouldn't end pretty on this chick's end. We weren't 'bout no games, and I was itching to unleash a good ass whooping on anybody that wanted it. The waitress peered in another direction and changed her tune before clicking her heels, going back to where she came from.

Cardi B's voice blared through the speakers on que, bringing Lexi and Sage to their feet in unison. I laughed as they snapped their fingers, mouthing the words to *Bodak Yellow* in the direction of the snooty waitress. They both made their way to the dance floor, looking like some old-ass thots tryna blend in.

It's been ages since I've been in the club V.I.P. section, but I must say, never was it as live and colorful as this. This spot is hot, the music is on point, the vibe and everything about it spoke volumes. I stood and looked over everyone else who was partying and having a good time. But tonight, all eyes were on me.

"Excuse me, Miss..." a voice came from behind. I stifled a sigh and continued sipping my Long Island as the man stopped at my table. I stirred my straw as I looked past him.

"You rocked that stage tonight, let me...."

"No, thank you."

"Damn, let me finish, ma." He chuckled annoyingly.

I cringed at the word *ma*. I hated when a grown man called me that almost as much as I hated seeing their pants hang beneath their asses.

"I couldn't help but—"

"I'm good...."

The man turned his nose up as if he had smelled his own breath. I had lost interest after smelling that shit inches away.

"Why you gotta be a —"

I raised my eyebrows before turning my pitiless glare towards him. "I don't think you wanna finish that statement. I would hate to have to waste my favorite drink by re-coloring that crisp white shirt you rockin'."

The man got ready to lean in. The grin on his face faded to a sneer. I grabbed my drink, waiting for him to move another inch, so I could follow through with my threat. He must've read my mind because he held his hands up and backed away. I rolled my eyes and picked up my glass, downing the last of my drink.

"We can't keep meeting like this," a familiar voice said before walking around me from behind. I looked at the man, the same man that was ogling at me when I was on the stage.

"I don't know what you are talking about; I don't even know you," I added, hunching my shoulders.

"You are correct; even though you rode in my car for damn near an hour, we were never really formally introduced. My name is C.J., and you are?"

"Not interested," I countered, raising my glass, giving him a cheer.

The sound of my phone was so loud, I almost rolled out of my bed. I reached over to the nightstand, knocking things over, trying to retrieve my cell.

"It's too damn early in the morning for you to be calling me, Sage," I answered groggily.

"How did it go? I was just making sure yo ass wasn't tied up nowhere after you insisted on your old friend taking you up to your room."

"What the hell are you talking about?" I asked, trying to remember what went down last night.

"I'm talking about that fine ass night club owner you had a nightcap with…which, might I add, I don't ever recall you telling me about."

My eyes darted around the room, searching for some clue that could help me put together the events that took place. I pulled the covers back. I was wearing a pair of pink boy shorts and a cami that I didn't remember changing into.

"You got nasty, didn't you, ole skank?"

"No, no… I did not!" I snapped, trying to convince myself more than I was her.

The key being inserted into my door was all the confirmation I needed. I cursed myself at the thought that I had brought this man home, and I can't even remember how it all went down.

"Sage," I said, speaking into the phone. "Let me call you back," I whispered, hanging up in Sage's face.

The door opened, and…

"Oh, Hell Naw… Jamel?"

Dontae

Times Up!

I USED THE KITCHEN counter to pull myself up. With every grunt and groan, I was introduced to a crushing pain. I used my free hand to find a towel to soak up the blood. I made my way over to the front door. The end of my garage seemed so damn far away. I stood in the doorway and checked my pants for my car keys.

Shit," I hissed, remembering I had lost my damn ride gambling.

"They gone give me my shit back," I mumbled, almost losing my balance.

I gripped the stairwell tightly as every step I took was slow and calculated. As soon as I reached the bottom of the stairs, I crumpled to the pavement in exhaustion. Glancing towards the end of the block, I looked around for someone, some inkling that could give me a ray of hope before I had lost too much blood. I pulled myself up again, mustering up the strength to take another step, and another and another. The blood pounded in my head as I staggered my way down the dark block. The crushing pain in my abdomen and my chest sent me hurling over as I coughed up blood. I stopped in my tracks, losing my vision. Everything had become blurry. I attempted to catch my breath; It felt as if all the air had been sucked from my body. No longer able to hold myself up, I could feel my body give way beneath me.

I knew it was only a matter of time before the grim reaper would capture my soul. My horrifying past had become my current reality. A reality that was now my life. I hated myself for becoming such a monster. I wanted so badly to turn back time, but my time was up! I struggled to keep my eyes open. I tried to scream out, say something, but it was too late.... My eyes became heavy as my mother's screams sent cold chills through my body.

"Stooop!!! Please let me go, Jonathan!"

I tossed and turned in my bed. I smothered my head with the pillows, trying to drown out the throbbing sobs of my mother. I sat up and pulled my knees into my chest. With every thud, my stomach churned. I rolled out of my bed and tip-toed my way into the tiresome disaster. A disaster that resounded through my skull with every slur that came out of my stepfather's drunken voice. Every swear word he spat sent butterflies into my gut as I stood there dreading the end of the song. I hated myself for allowing one man to put so much terror inside of me. I feared him for so long, too long. I had allowed this man to hurt the woman who had birth me, protected me, taught me the importance of defending myself. I pounded my fist into my head. 'How could I be so selfish?' I thought to myself.

"Shut the hell up!" *The angry growl bellowed through my walls.*

Her screams had quieted to whimpers. Eventually, everything went silent. I stuck my head out of my bedroom door, only to be introduced to my stepfather's fist smashing into my head. Dazed, I slumped against the wall, blood radiating slowly down my forehead. He went to strike me again, but this time, I caught his fist and gripped it tightly, locking eyes with him. I used every bit of strength inside of me to back him into a corner. I was no longer that ten-year-old that he could overpower. This time I was 17 years old and his height, if not taller. Although my mother would beg me to stay out of it, tonight, she had no say so. I turned to look in her direction, and she was balled into a corner, covered in blood, filled with scrapes and bruises.

After so many years, I didn't understand why my mother wouldn't leave him alone. It overwhelmed me, taunted me, and this day, I was overpowered by rage. Where the hell was my own father? Why had he left me, chose another child over me? Why hadn't he come to save my mother and me from this monster that haunted us in the wee hours of his drunken nights? With each thought that ran through my mind, I struck him, pounding into his face. My mother's cries were drowned out as I continued to beat this man who had raised me from the age of two.

"Stoooopp! Dontae! You're going to kill him!" My mother pleaded as she attempted to grab my arm. I shunned her off, sending her flying across the room. Stopping in my tracks, I ran over to her as I bent over to help her up. She outstretched her hand, sending a slap across my face so hard I almost forgot she was my mother.

"Leave!" She roared.

"What? But Ma..."

"Now!!!!!" She screamed louder, pushing me away.

My eyes burned as I watched my mother turn her face away from me. She refused to look at me until I turned to walk away. I got halfway to the door and turned around, only to find her consoling the very man that I thought I was protecting her from.

"There's blood everywhere. There's no way someone could lose that much blood and still be alive," a voice whispered softly.

"Go see if he's breathing," another voice mumbled.

"Why me?"

"Forget it, I'll go."

I gasped for air as someone put pressure on my wound.

"We have to get him to a hospital."

TY NESHA

"Let's just wait for the ambulance to arrive. They should be here any minute. I don't even think we should be standing here. We don't know what kind of trouble he's got himself into."

"Well, I'm not going to just leave him here."

The sound of sirens interrupted their conversation. I could hear all sorts of hustling and rustling. I tried to open my eyes, but they were so heavy. I could hear them gather around me before loading me onto the gurney and rushing me into the ambulance. I listened to the sound of my neighbors gathering around the scene.

"Where the hell were they when I was making my way down this dark ass street?" I thought to myself.

"Hold on sir. We...." Their voices began to fade as I was starting to lose consciousness.

"We have to get him over to County..."

"He's lost a lot of blood."

"We're losing him."

"Sir, stay with us."

"Clear..."

Darkness...

"Time of...."

Silence.

Boyfriend Number Two

"**P**lease don't tell me…"

"Baby, I can explain."

"Explain how you weaseled your way into my hotel room, Jamel. Explain that. You know what? I had to have been lit as hell to have let yo' ass up and in…"

I stood outside the door, amused at the commotion going on inside Love's suite. I couldn't bear letting her believe she took this cat home wit' her last night, so I decided to take her out of her misery and intervene. I took the key out of my back pocket with my free hand and pushed my way in with a bit of humor.

"Room service," I teased with a cunning smirk spread across my face.

"I'll take that," the dude insisted. I locked eyes with him briefly before turning to Love.

"Nah, you can leave, homie," I stated calmly, keeping my eyes on hers, savoring the complete shock on her face.

"Who the fuck are you?"

Ignoring him, I brushed past him, placing the breakfast on the nightstand. I leaned into her, playing into my role rather well, I must say.

"How'd you sleep, baby doll?" I asked, planting a soft kiss on her forehead.

Her mouth was in an 'o' shape as she ran her eyes around the room in disbelief.

"Oh, it's like that, Love?"

"You still standing there? I thought I asked you to bounce." This time, I spoke with more authority, glaring into his direction. I already knew how this shit was gone play out. A lot of folk let my looks fool them and....

"So, you fucking this Pretty Ricky, boyfriend number two looking ass clown, Love?"

I chuckled because it never failed. My smooth and debonair looks always gave people a reason to have me fucked up. In turn, it always ended with me fucking them up. I really ain't have time for that today, not in front of the lady.

I walked over to him and stood neck to neck with him as I lifted my collar and tilted my head to the side. I leaned into him and spoke to him in a stern undertone. "Don't let my Pretty Ricky ass looks fool you, homeboy. You really don't want these problems," I warned through clenched teeth. I smoothed out his collar before backing back a bit. "Besides. I don't play number two. Aint' no goin' behind this, patna," I taunted, groping my penis.

He nodded his head and stroked his chin while placing the hotel key at the edge of the bed.

"I see how it is. You can have her. I don't want her fat ass, no way. I just came to tell her Raelyn, and I were gone make this shit official since she having my shorty and all."

I could feel the room heating up as I tried my hardest not to break this boy's jaw. The room fell silent. Within moments, I could hear Love rising up from her bed. She walked over towards him, revealing the pain in her eyes as she stood in front of him. She removed the ring from her finger and placed it in his hand calmly.

54

"Get out!" She scoffed before slapping fire from his face.

His plan had backfired, and from the look on his face, he knew better than to strike back. Instead, he turned and walked away, slamming the door behind him.

Love stared into space. I could see the torrent of tears attack her. Her knees buckled, and she fell to the floor, burying her face into her hands.

It took me over an hour to console this woman. That's after convincing her that she wasn't a slut, and she hadn't slept with me in the heat of one of her drunken spells. Her homegirls were like two raging pit bulls at the thought of me even walking her into the hotel. They had gathered every bit of information from me damn near down to my dick print before letting me take her up. We had convinced them that we were old friends, and after Love insisted they "let her be great," they let up a bit. But not before that feisty one threatened to blow my whole establishment up if even a hair was touched on Love's head. Once we got up to the room, Love threw up all over the bathroom floor. I remained a gentleman, placed her into the shower, cleaned her up, and carried her to bed.

Now, I'm a man, and I would be lying if I said my manhood ain't jump a time or two, especially since her ass kept groping it. I don't have an issue with getting sex from a woman, so I'd rather wait until a lady was in their right mind before I went to stick my penis in 'em, you feel me?

I glanced down at this beautiful woman lying in my arms and wondered, *what if....* I shook the thought from my mind as she adjusted her body into mines. My body responded by hardening against hers. My large 6'2 stature swallowed her tiny 5'1 thick frame. My fingers traveled up her spine as she arched

55

her back into me. Turning her to her back, I mounted my body over hers. My eyes examined her as she lay there in noticeable heat. I used my hands as my tour guide to her sweet aroma; she was wet, soft, and responsive. She squirmed as my fingers danced around in her boy shorts. She grabbed my hands, aborting my mission.

"I can't…" she whispered, closing her eyes.

The sexual tension in the room was high, but all I needed was one time for a woman to tell me no. I don't play them "no means yes" games. A brotha got too much to lose.

"I understand," I whispered, lifting myself up.

She grabbed my face and brought it to hers. "I need it," she said with a look of desperation in a sexy kinda way. She gripped my manhood as it pulsated in her hands.

"You sure?"

She nodded her head in confirmation. I leaned into her, lodging my lips onto hers. She bit my bottom lip and released soft moans into my ear.

I pulled down her boy shorts with delicacy. She lifted her butt from the bed, allowing me complete access. I parted her legs and rubbed my fingers across her love box. Using my free hand, I reached over to my nightstand, grabbed my wallet, pulled out a rubber, and opened it with my teeth.

"You want it, put it on," I commanded, handing her the rubber.

She gave me a crafty grin before taking the rubber and working it on me. I gripped her legs, spreading them apart, now entering her slowly.

"Sssss…" she gasped, digging her nails into my back.

"Does it hurt?" I asked, still making my way inside her.

"Don't stop," she whispered in my ear, wrapping her lips around my earlobe.

Her walls tightened around my girth as I slid in and out of her, slow and steady. The way my manhood filled her insides made me feel like she was Cinderella, and my penis was the glass slipper that was a custom fit. She grimaced as I slid inside of her. With each stroke, she matched my rhythm. I could tell that the pain was turning into pleasure as she moaned loudly. She grabbed the pillow and covered her face to suppress the uncontrollable sounds that left her. I grinned cockily as I grabbed the pillow from her face. With every inch she tried to run, I pulled her in closer. Her moans were soft and needy as I fingered her clit simultaneously. She moved in time with me, driving her hips into my hand.

"Don't stop," she moaned.

I continued until I could feel her body stiffen as she began to jerk. I pulled myself out of her and dove my face into her vagina. She fidgeted uncontrollably as my tongue made love to her clit until she came into my mouth. I kept at it until her legs shook in satisfaction.

She looked down at me with a grin spread across her face. "A man cannot discover new oceans until he's lost sight of the shore." She chuckled before throwing her head back, letting out a deep breath.

"Touché, my Love, touché."

I grabbed my cell phone off the night table, where it buzzed. I looked over at Love, and she was sound asleep. The two weeks we spent together had flown by. I must admit, I was enjoying every bit of it. The chemistry between us was undeniable. It was something about this woman that made me want to get to know her more and more. I kissed her on the forehead before I arose from the bed and silently walked over to the window.

"Dom, what's good?" I answered.

"We got a problem," he said, and my heart stopped briefly.

"Oh yea?" I whispered, looking back at Love resting peacefully.

"Yea but…" There was a brief silence.

"Dom? What's wrong, bruh?"

"I need you to come to County hospital. I found your brother. It's bad, Chris, really bad."

Alexis

What's Done in the Dark

I WAS HURLED OVER in pain, laughing so hard from listening to Love break down how things played out "the morning after."

"He said what?"

"Girl, yes! He knows I'm sensitive about my damn weight."

"Wait, so you mean to tell me after all that he said, that's what hurt the most?"

"Hell yea! I'm going to the gym first thing in the morning too," she attested as she continued smacking in my ear.

"Girl forget his, Tyrese reject looking ass. He got some nerve, running around here looking like a repeat episode of 'what more do you want from me?' I wish his broke ass would call somebody out of their name. I would've eaten his ass for dinner if I were you, just for the hell of it." I jabbed as I rolled my eyes.

"Well damn, Lex. Tell me how you really feel."

"I'm just saying, you know damn well I ain't never liked Jamel. His broke ass always had his hand out but dared to walk around here stuntin' like he was the man. That boy was living a rapper's lifestyle on a McDonald's budget."

59

TY NESHA

I could go on and on about Loves poor choices in men. She always gravitated towards the broke bum dudes too. It's like she got a kick outta saving these grown boys or something. She always hollered out how she wanted a man that had the basics. You know, the simple shit like a car, a job, and a place to live.

As simple as it sounded, the crazy thing is that men like that, black men, black men who actually wanted to date another black woman, yea, well, them brothas, were rare and far in-between. I always say, 'If I'm rocking with a dude, best believe he is doing something for me. These females gone learn one day to quit entertaining dudes that won't buy you a happy meal!!'

And every time she met a man, a man that had his shit together, she would push them away and then turn right around and end up with a dude laying up in her shit, playing video games and smoking up her paycheck.

But what do I know? Here I am, 21 years old, still busting down tables. I smoothed out my uniform and stared at my reflection through the window. I had a look that most of these females would pay for. My dark brown wavy hair was in disarray as it fell past my shoulders, my work uniform had all sorts of stains, exposing how my day went, and even in my most rugged moment, there still wasn't a chick in these streets that could hold a candle to me. People would always say I resembled Melanie Fiona, and based on the number of times I would get stopped in the streets, I would have to agree. Having a celebrity look-alike had its perks too. It got me tons of free stuff just for a picture or a fake ass autograph. I know this much; with these looks, there was no way in hell I should be busting down tables for tips. I appreciated Love helping me get a job and all, but I was two seconds away from walking out on my day job and taking my homegirl, Jersei, that's Jersey, with an I, up on her offer. Moving to L.A. didn't sound like a bad idea, especially since this Chicago weather was so damn

60

bipolar. I looked out the window as the snowflakes hit the pavement.

"Lexi, do you hear me talking to you?" Love snapped, taking me out of my somber daydream.

"I hear you, Love. I just don't want you to get hurt, that's all."

"What the hell are you talking about? I was telling you I passed my exam. I'm so close to finishing law school, I can taste it."

"Oh girl, my bad. I'm so happy for you," I said, trying to convince her that I really was happy. Inside I just wanted to make it to the top and surpass her and Sage just so I can say I did it.

"I just don't understand why you would go to the man's house, Lex. Why you always gotta act on impulse, sis? Damn!"

Impulsive wasn't the word to describe my antics, actions, or even the motive behind why I did what I did. At first, I felt justified. Then, I felt like Dontae's ass had me messed up if he would think he could just write me off like I was just some regular-ass female. It served him right, hell. Who knew his wife wasn't able to tell the difference between a fake ultrasound and a real one. Oh, yea, I forgot she can't have kids anyway; let Tae tell it.

"Well, I told his ass not to keep on playing with me. I don't know why these dudes always wanna test my crazy."

I could hear Sage's ole bougie ass take an exasperated breath over the phone. "You know how I feel about this side chick life, but if you must be about that life, please understand there are levels to this shit."

"Well, I'm on a level on my own," I stated, smacking my lips.

Look, y'all, you can say what you want about a side chick. How a woman that will settle for second place has no self-worth and all that nonsense. So, tell me this, why is it that me, as a "side chick," gets treated better than his woman? And let's talk about self-worth. What kind of self-worth does a woman who continues to take a man back, cheating on her continuously, have? In my mind, I'd prefer this life, this way. I controlled these men the way I wanted to, and I always had something over their heads. I play the game; I don't get played. On top of that, it's just something about being underestimated that turns me on. How the woman is just oblivious to the fact that I fuck the shit outta her man every chance I got.

"I'd rather be on this end than sitting up at 4 am wondering what level in someone's house my man landed on."

There was a long silence; I couldn't take it back; it was already said.

"Sage. My bad, I didn't…."

"Nah, you right. His lying ass ain't come home last night either."

"You lying."

"Nope, but it's cool," she said nonchalantly.

"Wait, you sound like you smiling. Why the hell are you smiling? We ain't bout to go do a drive-by or nothing, are we?"

"Heck no!" I could hear a different Sage on the other end of the receiver. She was jovial and less apprehensive.

"Sage?"

"Well… Don't say shit, Lexi."

"Who the hell to, Sage?"

I could hear her take a deep break before letting the cat out of the bag. "I met someone."

I clamped my mouth shut.

"Hello, say something. I can't believe it. For the first time in history, Alexis Harris, silent."

"Well, looks to me like history is on a roll. My bougie friend got two men tasting her cookies."

"Hell no! Me and Gavin ain't slept together in months."

"Months! No wonder why the man ain't coming home, girl."

"Nah, he been doing this for years. My ass just kept making excuses and wishing he wasn't out there, acting like sharing is caring. I caught his ass up so many times, I just fell numb to it. He paid my way through medical school and...."

"And what? You owe him?"

"It's not that, it's just now he's outta work, and tryna get back on his feet. I didn't wanna kick the man while he was down."

"All along, he all over town kicking down bitches' walls.... hell Nah, him not having nothin' is even more reason for you to bounce."

"Yea, I feel you," she said. "Look, I gotta go. I'll hit you up later."

I hung up the phone and turned my attention to something more deserving. I turned my key in the door and twisted the knob, entering my new place.

I walked over to the edge of the bed, careful not to wake the fine piece of chocolate that lay before me. Out of all of the men I had dealt with, he was the only one that was able to break down the walls to my heart. I rubbed my belly softly. I knew it was only a matter of time before I started showing; people would start asking questions and.... I blew into the air in frustration. I pretended to be this skanky whore just to keep people from uncovering the truth about us. After all, how could I explain this? *"This"* wasn't supposed to happen. He was

63

my first everything. No one would ever know that, and that's how I liked it. People speculated but never really knew the men that had been in between these thighs. I was careful; I chose wisely. And no matter who came into my life, in the end, I chose him. He knew it, and so did I. To us, that's all that mattered.

"Everything is going to work out fine, Lexi. Just be patient." I couldn't tell you how many times I had heard those words. We had been playing this game since I was 17, four years and the same ole story. Eventually, patience wears thin and what's in the dark comes to light.

I walked into the bathroom and filled a cup with cold water. I took a sip and stood over him as I watched him sleep in peace. I removed the cup from my lips slowly, appreciating the way it quenched my thirst. I took one more sip and threw the water onto his face.

"What the…."

"So, yo' ass ain't go home last night, Gavin?"

The Dark Angel

"So, how long he been here?"

"A few weeks."

"A few weeks? Dom, how the hell we just now finding out, though?"

"It just hit my desk this morning. I asked the same question."

"You think?"

"Nah? Them cats he owes, they would've killed him. This was somebody he trusted that did this. Somebody that..."

I looked at my brother through the glass window as he fought for his life, barely hanging on and hooked up to numerous machines. Even though Dontae was older than me, I made a vow to do whatever I could to keep him out of harm's way from the moment I found out I had a brother. I don't know if it was because I had nobody that was there for me or if it was just the cloth I was cut from. I always knew my brother had resentment towards me, and although I hated some of his ways, I still felt I owed it to him to give him the security neither of us had. Dontae wanted to trade places with me so bad, he never understood why our father would turn his back on one son and embrace the other. I chuckled at *embrace*. People think just because you were raised up in a big house and lots of money, you ought to be grateful; disregard anything that came with the price of....

"Get in the car, boy, now!" My father screamed, shoving me into the stretched limo.

"Christopher, no! Where are you taking him? Please, don't do this!" My mother screamed as she ran down the stairs of our home. Her black lace gown dragged against the ground, kissing the puddles with every step she took in our direction.

I planted the palm of my hand against the window and yelled for her, but she couldn't hear me.

"Why are you doin' this? Why are you taking my boy?" The sobs left her mouth as one of his goons grabbed her from behind, holding her back.

"You don't want me here, right? Well, I'm going, but if I go, he goes too. Chris is just as much my son as he is yours. A woman doesn't know the first thing about raising a boy into a man. Hell, a woman can't raise a boy to be a man, period; let alone, a white woman ain't got no business tryna bring up a boy of color in this world alone."

"We can do it together. We don't have to be to..."

"It's been decided. You want 'em, come get him. Let's see how that plays out for you." My father chuckled.

"He's just a boy. All he needs is...."

"Is what, Rachel? To be babied, coddled, sheltered from the world, the reality in which he must live in. Leaving him here with you is nothing but a setup, a setup for my boy to remain oblivious to the fact that who he is has nothing to do with what he looks like. The fact that he can be taken out by his own or gunned down like some animal by someone that looks just like you."

At nine years old, I didn't understand what my father meant. Why would he think someone would hurt me just by the way I looked?

My father walked around to the other side and opened his door.

"He needs his father!"

The tears erupted from my mother's face as she snatched away from my dad's goon. She ran over to the car and placed her tiny hands on the other side of the window to match mines.

"You see that, baby?" She said, referring to the inside of her hand and mines. "No matter what we look like on the outside… inside, we are all the same. Don't you ever forget that, baby. Don't you ever let anyone tell you that you are beneath them because of what you look like. You can conquer the world if you want to. You are a boss, Christopher James, and don't you ever forget that."

"Let me out!" I screamed as I pulled the handle to the door. It wouldn't open, so I banged on the windows.

"I'm coming back for you, baby. I promise, I'm coming back."

"Aye, ain't yo' brother married?" Dom asked, taking me out of my reverie.

"Yea, but Desi, she wouldn't hurt a fly."

"Well, don't be so sure about that. One of the nurses said there was a lady that was brought in shortly before your brother. They say she was beaten up pretty badly and on suicide watch. The blood on her clothes didn't come from her, C.J."

"Nah man," I said, shaking my head dismissively.

"Well, only one way to find out," he retorted, walking down the hall. I could feel a lump form in my throat. I didn't want this to be the case. I mean, I wouldn't say that I'd blame Desi for not wanting to allow Dontae to keep putting his hands on her. I just….

"You coming, or nah?"

I put some pep in my step and followed him down the hall. We got to the door, and I froze in time, not even wanting to see this woman in here all jacked up and out of sorts. Dom tapped lightly on the door before pushing it open.

"Excuse me, you can't be back here, sir."

"I'm sorry, it's just, I'm looking for this woman. Have you seen her here?" I asked, showing the nurse a picture from Desiree's Facebook profile.

The nurse looked at the picture and shook her head, handing me back the phone. "No, not familiar. But, let me ask my sub. I just started my shift twenty minutes ago, and I'm just now returning from leave. Betty, come here a sec!" She called out, waving the older lady to come in our direction.

"What's up, chile?"

"You seen this girl around here?" She asked, reaching for me to give her my phone.

She took the phone and passed it to Betty. "Who's asking?" She said, shifting her eyes up to me and then to Dom.

"I'm detective Dominick Hayes, and this here is her brother. We just want to make sure she's ok."

"Lil too late for that," she said, handing me back the phone.

"Her husband checked her out a few hours ago."

"Her husband?" I asked, looking at Dom in confusion.

"Yep. I went to go draw up her discharge papers, and by the time I got back, they both had vanished. I call her The Dark Angel. That child was so angelic in her own right, but I learned a long time ago, even angels have demons."

The Lion's Den

I COULD SEE THE tears accumulate in her eyes until they were full enough to fall down her face. I drove in silence; whoever had instilled so much fear inside this woman had to be inhumane. I despised a man that felt he had to use an iron fist to control the mind of a woman. It's never that fucking serious, man. I headed towards my spot that I had out south 69th and Jeffrey.

"Where are we going?" She whispered groggily.

"Somewhere safe," I assured her, turning into the parking garage.

I carried her into my spot. She nestled her head into my chest like she had known me forever. I wasn't with all that mushy shit, but she reminded me so much of Love. Whenever Love was broken down, she'd always burrow her head into me until she would fall fast asleep. I hated how I had failed her. I wished that I could turn back the hands of time, but shit didn't always work out the way we intended them to. I had gotten so wrapped up in my own shit, I hadn't even been there for my sister. Had it not been for me, shit may be different for her.

Four Years Prior

I walked into the spot and heard the most heavenly voice coming from the front room. I placed the groceries on the kitchen counter and made my way to the most divine singing I had ever heard. Hands down, my sister could out sing any singer in the industry, only if she'd believed that herself.

"Why you tryna sneak up on me, Kane Wright?" She asked as she rubbed her protruding belly.

"Ain't sneaking on nothing, Love. Just enjoying the show," I replied, now placing my hand on her shoulders. "I don't know why you won't just let J.R. record you in his studio. He said..."

Love took an exasperating breath. "Kane, I already told you that ain't my thing. I'm trying to get my Law degree, and I don't need any distractions. About a month from now, this little one gone have a new family and..."

"Love! You mean to tell me you still going through with that? After all the..."

"Kane, I don't know one thing about being a mom. With you always out and the daddy..."

"Fuck her daddy! I'm the daddy," I countered, raising my voice.

Before I could finish my argument, Love doubled over in pain.

"You ok?" The look on her face terrified me, sending me into a panic.

The splash on the wooden floors frightened me even more.

"What the hell was that?"

"I think my water just broke, Kane. This baby is coming...NOW!"

My squad and I were all two-time felons, and after careful consideration, I did what any real man would do. I put my whole team on. We invested in properties that we knew we could reconstruct for the low. These were properties that no other agencies wanted parts of because of the reputations of the neighborhoods. In a year, instead of working the street corners, I owned them. I had even put enough money to the side to invest in Love's law degree. She wouldn't dare take a handout from me, no matter how much I tried to convince her. So, I added her name to the company as part owner. She still insisted on working at the restaurant "just in case." I had everything figured out until I got served papers that one of the condo residents had fallen due to negligence and was suing the agency. They were trying to take Wright's Realty to the cleaners, and I had no idea how I would get out of this without getting my hands dirty. Imagine my surprise when I got word a cat I use to provide muscle for back in the day had a business venture for ya mans. I knew this was just what I needed to clear up all my issues and get back to work.

"This here is the business opportunity I had for you, Kane," he stated as we walked through his spot.

"I'm not following. I mean, no shade to you, man, but the club thing is not for me."

"Kane, how long have we known each other? Don't answer that," he said. "Have a seat." He pointed toward the barstool aside from me.

"On this day three years ago, I had just walked away from a position of power. The streets got me paid, but in turn, there was no love there, only envy and greed. It was only a matter of time that all my dirt would catch up to me, and it would end with me in a box or behind a cell. Bondage was never my thing, so I chose to change the game. They can take everything from you, but one thing they could never take is your mind. That's why this," he said, tapping his head. "The mind is a monster; you just gotta feed it. No matter what they take, they can never take away your intellect. I left Boston, washed my hands of the streets, and came back here starting from scratch. I was broke, no job, sleeping on an air mattress in my homeboy's studio. Two years later, here we are."

He walked around the bar and looked at me pointedly, his eyes serious.

"We, you, and me. We are the Lions, and this is our den." He pulled down the projection screen, exposing the large blueprint.

"So many people fail to see the bigger picture, but not me. I'm looking to expand. But I need someone with an empire-building mindset. From the day I met you outside of them projects tryna hustle me down to my socks, I knew that one day I would need a brother with that kind of determination and dedication on my squad."

"I'm flattered. I really am, but I don't work for no one, man. I'm my own…"

"Boss." He added, finishing my statement.

"Indeed, you are. And I don't think anything less of you. You ever heard the saying, 'Give a man a fish, and you feed him for a day?"

"Teach a man to fish, and you feed him for a lifetime," we both spoke in unison.

"What you did with your partners shows me your character. You are not only a leader, but you are loyal. How you revamped those project houses and poured into those youth centers in those neighborhoods shows me you are tenacious. You know how to orchestrate things and create revenue, all while feeding your team."

The things he was saying, I already knew. I remained humble and listened to him, studied him, the way he moved, spoke and the fact that he had done the same to me spoke volumes. I nodded as he spoke. I took it all in, now knowing where he was going with things. I looked down at the blueprints; the plan was immaculate, a mastermind. If we did this right, we would have our own version of a Rosemont in no time, but bigger and better.

"Today, this is just club Finesse. Eventually, it will become so much more. This is going to be a major milestone, a movement. A representation of that will become the brand for

72

brothers like you and me; whatever doesn't kill us only makes us stronger; The Lion's Den!"

We both smiled and nodded our heads in unison.

"I'm not looking for an employee, Kane. I'm looking for a partner. And you, my man, are it. I'm just tryna feed you and eat for a lifetime."

Sage

My Cup Runneth Over

"If I could, could forget him
I would, please believe me.
And I know that I should throw the towel in
But baby, it's not, not that easy......"

JAZMIN SULLIVAN'S VOICE BLARED through the speakers of my headphones, serenading my whole entire life. I flushed the toilet and washed my hands to give the impression that I was in the bathroom for its intended purpose. My phone chimed again as I walked back to the den.

'Looking forward to tonight. Are we still on?'

I wanted more than anything to spend a night on the town with this man, but I needed to figure out how to make it work. I heard the footsteps coming in my direction. I sent a quick response before putting my phone on DND.

'Not sure. I'll text you tonight.' I smiled and deleted our messages. I turned around to see Gavin standing in the walkway, sipping his drink. I picked up the small bag that rested by my feet.

"Where you off to, Sage?" He asked. His light brown eyes stared into mines. I used to look in those eyes and get all tingly

74

inside. I gazed a little harder, just to see if I could feel something, anything. There was nothing.

"I'm going over to Lexi's. She needs help unpacking, so...."

"Lexi's, huh?" He said, stroking his chin.

Before I could respond, his phone pinged, thankfully giving me a perfect out before I would tell another lie. As he looked down at his phone, I tried to brush past him. He put his arm out and wrapped it around my waist, pulling me into him. When his phone chimed again, he glanced at the text and cleared his throat.

"I told you I don't like you hangin' with that girl, Sage," he said, putting his full lips on my neck.

"And I told *you* she is my friend. I don't know why you have such an issue with Lexi, Gavin."

He let go of my waist and took a step back. "That girl ain't yo' friend. That's yo' problem. You think all these hoes is your..."

"Hoes? What we not gone do is call my sister..."

"Oh. So, is she ya friend or ya sister, Sage?" He asked with a sarcastic chuckle.

"Both!" I retorted, staring into his eyes. He had taken me from zero to ten in a matter of seconds.

"What's your gripe, Gavin? You don't see me walking around here complaining about what you choose to do and who you choose to roll wit. Every time yo' ass stay out all night, or just so happen to fall asleep with one of yo' guys..."

"Oh, so that's what this is about. Me staying out? I already told you..."

I threw my hands up. "Listen, I don't even care no more. You do what it is you wanna do. I refuse to sit up all night worried about a man that can't even recognize a real woman when he has her."

"Oh, so we wanna talk about a real woman, do we? Tell me this, Sage. Why is it that my woman, the real woman that she is, can't even reproduce a child for her man?"

I froze in time. He did not just say that to me. He did not just... I could feel the blood in my body rushing straight to my head. I tried to bite back what was gone escape from my mouth, but this man has lost his damn mind. I clutched the strap of my bag and threw it over my shoulder. I removed my keys from the pocket and narrowed my eyes in his direction. I walked close enough to him that I could stick my tongue down his throat.

"Oh, baby, know this... if I wanted to reproduce, I could push triplets out my ass right now if I wanted to. Don't get it twisted, playa. This ain't that. I wouldn't dare bring a baby in this world by a man that would rather lay up at his 'boys' house all night than with his woman. I wouldn't be surprised if..."

"If what?" He hissed, clenching his jaw. "Say it, and I'll lay yo' ass out right here in this room."

Gavin had never raised a hand to me, but he would talk shit all day. Still, I didn't take his idle threats lightly. In the back of my mind, I always knew. There are two kinds of men in the elevator, Jay Z and Ray Rice, and I ain't wanna be the one to toss the coin.

I pushed my brand-new Kia Soul down the Dan Ryan at 80 miles per hour. My mind was in a frenzy, and although I was over Gavin and his bullshit, it wasn't that simple to walk away. My cup runneth over with him so many times, and I just kept taking sips from it, just enough so I can see it as half full instead of the emptiness that it really was.

I met Gavin when I was fourteen years old. He was my best friend and my only friend back then. I never had girlfriends until now. They were too damn mischievous, in my opinion. I lost my virginity to him, and after that, my life changed.

"Pregnant? What do you mean pregnant?" My mother's eyes burned fire into my soul as I sobbed uncontrollably at the edge of my bed. I had taken myself to a walk-in clinic after having bad cramping pains in my stomach. I knew something wasn't right, and by the time I took action, I was already seven months, and I didn't even know it. They let me hear the baby's heartbeat and everything. The thing is, I always wore baggy clothes, and I thought the increase in my appetite was average. I hadn't even gained that much weight. My mother was enraged as she pulled out her phone and started punching numbers. Just as the voice came across the other end of the phone, mama stormed off, closing the door behind her. I listened intently to the hushed whispers, but I couldn't gather what she was saying. I walked to the door and placed my ear against it.

"Hell no! I am not bringing a damn baby into this house. I got enough mouths to feed."

"I need you to call the lady from that agency and see how we can draw up the papers for...."

"What else we gone do? It's too late for an abortion, Will." After hearing my father's name, I already knew this wasn't going to go over well. Her whispers became muffled, and the footsteps clicked back towards my direction. I hurried back over to my bed before the door swung open.

"Pack ya bags. You goin' to live with Grandma Jean for a while."

The police lights behind me took me out of my thoughts. I pulled over, cursing myself for not paying better attention. I watched out my rearview as the officer stepped out the unmarked vehicle and made his way to my window. He was a fine hunk of chocolate too. My heart did a little dance as I took in his grandiose stature. His slacks fit just right around his powerful thighs. He didn't wear a uniform, but his badge lodged against the leather Ferragamo belt buckle aligned through the loopholes of his pants. I observed the magnificent wall of muscle that stood outside my car window. There is just something about the uniform and being naughty that excites me. His coffee-brown skin had me licking my lips in approval. I pressed the button and rolled down my window as I removed my Dior shades from my face.

Get it together Sage. I thought.

"Is everything ok, officer?" I asked, keeping my hands on the steering wheel.

"Please step out of the vehicle, ma'am," he said, staring into my car. The resonance in his voice sent a penetrating heat flowing through my body.

"Did I do something wrong?" I asked, knowing I was driving like a bat out of hell.

"I'm not going to ask again. Step out of your car, please!" He ordered sternly, pulling my door open.

"Damn, he's an ass," I thought as I stepped out of my car slowly, keeping my hands where he could see them. He grabbed my arm and shoved me against the car.

"Sir, is there a reason…"

"I ask the questions here," the officer sneered, rubbing his hands down my legs sexually.

He snatched my body around to face him. His piercing dark brown eyes held my stare just as his lips cruised into mines. Since Mr. Dominick Hayes was an officer of the law, I didn't want to resist, so instead, I fell into compliance.

"Do you do this with all the civilians?' I asked, taking in the aroma of my favorite cologne.

He rubbed his fingers through my blonde hair and tilted my head back, kissing my neck.

"Not all! But you are definitely on my most wanted list."

I Surrender

I rushed into the restaurant with my three-year-old daughter in my arms, just in time for my shift.

"Love, what are you doing? Your shift starts in five minutes?" Vernice, my coworker, asked with her hands on her hips.

"I know, Vern. Kane was supposed to pick her up over an hour ago. I have been calling his phone, and he isn't answering," I said, placing my baby girl into the booth.

"Heyyyyyyyy, Tee Tee baby," Lexi said, coming out the back. She dove right in, smothering my little angel with kisses and tickles. "Yo' mama gone get fired for having you here. You know that, right?" She teased as she tickled my baby out of her jacket.

I smiled at my baby girl as she looked up at me with her big dough eyes, looking like a miniature china doll. Her hair was pulled back in a neat bun with a red, white, and blue headband that rested on her head like a little tiara.

"You already know it's the holiday, and Big Bennie is not gone care about nothing if I don't show up. I just need you to help me out until my brother calls me back. If I miss another day, he gone be pissed."

Lexi pursed her lips and picked up my daughter, smothering her with more kisses. "I'll take her to the back. She can watch Paw Patrol on my phone for a little while. Ain't that right?" She said in a high-pitched voice before they wandered off to the back.

I peered out of the window as two dudes hopped out of a black Lambo. I squinted my eyes to get a glimpse, but they moved swift and anxiously through the crowd.

The blaring from the horn startled me, causing me to spill the cup of coffee on my hot pink shirt, bringing me out of my thoughts. I rushed over to the window. "Here I come, man!" I yelled out. I grabbed a towel and blotted my shirt until I was satisfied enough to walk out the door.

I skipped down the stairs as my brother's fine self rested against his ride in a B-boy stance.

"Finally! You always were a slow poke," he teased before planting a kiss on my cheek and pulling open the passenger door. I rolled my eyes and poked out my lips before kissing him back.

"Look at you, looking all slim and trim. You been working out or something?" He asked jovially.

I smacked my lips and adjusted my shirt, looking down at my tummy to see if I noticed a change. "Don't be trying to butter me up. Don't think I forgot."

"Man, look, I said I was sorry."

"I know, but what makes you think you can just keep on beating up my boyfriends every time they do something stupid? I'm 30 years old now. I can handle myself, Kane."

Kane pulled off into the wind, sending me flying back in my seat. "Look, I already told your ass I ain't like dude no way, but you ain't wanna listen to ya big brother," he said pointedly.

I folded my arms like I used to when I was a little girl and turned my nose up. "Well, we ain't talked about how many of your trashy little girlfriends I ain't like, but I ain't go around beating them up, now did I?"

He shifted his eyes between me and the road. "That's cuz your ass can't fight."

. . .

We pulled up to the most beautiful condominiums hidden in plain sight along the glorious Chicago river.

"What you think?"

"Think about what?" I asked, still staring up at the enormous structure before me.

"Your new spot," he said, almost making me choke on my saliva.

"What, huh...wait. Kane, no! I...you. We... can't afford this," I said, stammering over my words.

"Says who?" He said, putting the car in park and exiting the vehicle.

By the time we made it into the front door, my brother had run down everything about his new business partner and how he put him up in this place, all expenses paid.

"I'm not moving in with you, Kane," I said assertively while I followed him through the condo.

"Of course, you're not. This ain't my type of party, sis. You know I feel more comfortable in something a lil less flashy," he chuckled. "You got surround sound in every room and even outside. You know how much you love singing. Now you can relax in the hot tub and enjoy the sunset. Here is the master bedroom, and this right here," he said, stepping aside. "Is the door that leads you right out to..."

"The deck!" I finished, astounded as I walked out onto the second-story deck and held onto the railing, taking in a deep breath, relishing in the cool breeze that whispered sweet melodies in my ear.

At that moment, I let out a long, liberating exhale as I submitted to the pleasures of unencumbered city living.

"I surrender," I whispered, closing my eyes modestly.

"I'm glad you like it," a deep voice thundered.

TY NESHA

I turned with a sharp twist, bringing my eyes up to the brotha in the doorway with a cunning grin planted on his face. I swallowed so hard, I could've ingested my tongue. I hadn't seen him in almost a month, but to see him today was a sight in itself. I just needed to know who was responsible for this; this man! See, this man wasn't a typical method of conception. There was some super extraordinary divine-ship that was in concoction with this man. Lord Jesus! He put me in the mind of that singer Ginuwine. His low cut and royal features were coated in toasted-toffee-colored skin that complimented perfectly with his gold-toned eyes. His body was carved to perfection. A body of a man that took pride in his physique encased in a gray Brook's Brother suit with a pink shirt underneath. *"Not only is he ridiculously handsome, but the man can wear the hell out of a suit and tie."* I thought, licking my lips lustfully.

"C.J., you made it," my brother said enthusiastically, interrupting my little mental molestation period.

"This is my baby sister, Love. Love, this is my new business partner, C. J."

The Incident

"I think we've met before," I said with a devilish grin.

I could see her turn bloodshot red as she choked on the wine I had poured for her.

"She sang at the club about a month ago," I continued.

"What? Hell no! She doesn't like singing in front of people," Kane said shockingly, pulling his sister into him.

Love gave an embarrassing smile before taking a big gulp from her glass.

"I can't believe I missed that."

"You missed one hell of a show. I would love for her to *come* again," I said, putting a strong emphasis on *come*.

Although most people view me as a serious businessman, my whit and silly ways were just naturally my character. I must admit, when I first saw Kane entering the penthouse with Love, I just knew he and her were an item. The way she leaned into him when she laughed and smiled when he spoke to her. The last few times I'd seen her, she was so somber and broken. The energy she entailed with Kane gave her a raving glow, but I could still see the brokenness in her eyes; I can't hide that. The day I left her, I had rushed out so fast, I hadn't even had the chance to get her number. I went back to the hotel, and she was checked out.

I stood aside for a second, watching her and Kane ramble about how he didn't have to do this and so forth. The sibling love they had was something I'd lacked and had been searching for from the day I met Tae. I wished we could have had that bond as young boys growing up. The day they released him from the hospital, I insisted on him staying at my place while he was recovering. He was back to his old self in no time but insisted that he'd find Desiree and make her come back to him. Dominick hated the idea of me taking him in. Ever since I met Dontae, there was one incident or bailout after the next. Repeatedly, Dontae would brush it off and dismiss it, just like our father......leading up to "The Incident."

"Heads High...kill them with the No! Just make a bwoy know you nah blow

Heads High...kill them with the No! No bwoy ain't got no secret for you...Heads High." No *matter how Americanized I was, my Jamaican roots were engrained deep inside my soul, and the rude boy in me just remained dormant more times than others.*

I pulled up across from Bennie's Barbeque joint, letting my reggae music blast through my speakers. Dontae leaned in to turn down the volume. My nostrils flared while I gave him a menacing glare. I hated when people touched my music, especially when I was in my zone. I leaned in myself and turned the volume off.

I investigated the inside of the joint through its window, making a mental note of the visible patrons and employees. Dom sat in one of the booths, pretending to flip through the newspaper. We waited patiently for him to take a sip from his coffee to indicate that it was safe for us to head up. Benny was turned sideways, appearing to be scolding one of his employers that I couldn't seem to get a clear vision of. Not only was Benny the owner of five of the best Barbeque and Soul food joints in the Chicago area, but he was also connected in ways one wouldn't imagine.

After some thorough investigation, I discovered that his son, Nasir, was behind the beating put on my brother weeks prior. Word was, Nasir was one of the most feared Loan Sharks in the area. I said feared, not respected. People only fear the unknown, and Nasir didn't put in work in these streets. He let others put in the work for him and being that Bennie was "The Plug," amongst other things, Nasir was grandfathered into this dirty game. But he wasn't cut enough to get dirty. I knew that from a personal level, which is why I sit here with a mixture of humor and disgrace rolled all in one. Nasir and I had history and our own little run-ins back in my day. One thing Nasir wasn't was about that one life. And he damn sure didn't want to feel my wrath.

"Is that them?" I asked my brother while gazing in the direction of Nasir and the three dudes heading towards the back of the barbeque joint.

"Hell yea." He nodded as he put fire to the blunt that rested between his lips.

I just nodded my head while downloading each image that walked behind that building, all while scoping the scene simultaneously. I reached into the glove compartment and grabbed my piece.

Though I used to be heavy in the streets, I really ain't have no interest in getting my hands dirty after my mom's passing. I figured that coming to the Chi could give me a clean slate and get me on track; that's exactly what I did. I gave up that one life, but I'd be lying if I told y'all I ain't still love the sound the Draco makes when you let it buss! Put the fear of GOD in a sucka. I guess the .45 will have to do, for now, I thought as I tucked it into my crisp white Levi's.

As we made our way into the two-story building, there was an eerie aura; murder lurked here. Images flicked through my head, and I shook them off, ignoring my instincts.

I sat firmly before Nasir and some of the most dominant gamblers in the streets of Chicago like I had an entourage of fifty men standing behind me.

"I hear you talking, C.J., but your brother owes me a lot of money. If I was to let that slide, what kind of message am I sending to the others? Surely a man of your caliber would understand the dilemma that stands before me; it's all about principle," Nasi stated contemptuously.

"Indeed, I do understand." I nodded, reaching into my breast pocket.

His goons cocked their guns, making my trigger finger itch, but I contained myself for the sake of the harmony I came for this day.

"No need for that. Stand down," he instructed, still gazing in my direction.

I continued with caution, pulling out an envelope. I sat it on the table and pushed it in his direction.

"It's all there," I assured him. "With interest," I added, my hand still on the envelope. "I need to know that my brother is going to be left alone indefinitely."

He nodded for one of his men to take the envelope. After counting the money, the goon shook his head in approval.

My hand rested on my waistline for access to my piece. I had to keep in mind that I was once an unruly savage that got a high off of raucous and mischief; I underestimated no one.

Nasir stood and extended his hand. I returned the gesture modestly.

Before I knew it, Dontae snapped, grabbing the big fella by the throat with one hand, lifting him off the ground. His goons and I upped our pieces in unison. A look of anger flicked in the eyes of Nasir. Our short-lived standoff was interrupted when another man entered the room. This dummy, Dontae, was supposed to be manning the door. Instead, he wanted to play "The Hulk" just for the hell of it. I went into autopilot mode, and in the blink of an eye, there were shots fired, and bodies dropped.... The unforeseen incident that followed left me to carry a burden heavy enough to lead me to self-destruction.

Dontae

The Company We Keep

"*What the hell happened up there?*" *Dom asked, pushing me against the wall.*

"*He lost his damn mind; that's what happened,*" *C.J. answered ragefully.*

"*What the hell were you thinking?*" *He screamed, pacing back and forth.*

Dom's phone rang, and he disappeared around the corner, leaving my brother and me alone to quarrel.

"*I was thinking, how in the hell were you just gone pay them niggas and let them breathe after what they did to me?*"

"*Tae, we had an understanding, man.*"

"*No, you did. I ain't agree to shit,*" *I countered with an immovable stare, humored at the fact that my new-found brother suddenly wanted to play the superman in the movie.*

"*So, you thought it was wise to put me and my freedom at risk?*"

"*As long as you are willing to face the consequences like a man, there is no such thing as a risk! I'm prepared to face the repercussions. That's what makes me different than you.*" *I jolted.*

87

"You picked a fine time to play hero, don't you think?" I asked, flaring my nostrils.

"The fuck you say to me?" He hissed, walking in my direction.

"You heard me."

C.J gritted his teeth as he pushed himself into me. Before things could escalate, Dom walked back into the room, his hand on his head. "One of the cats still breathing. For y'all, that may be a good thing. Get rid of the gun asap. I got to go back to the station and clean some shit up. The bad news is, one of the victims…"

I looked over at the news, and a picture of the most innocent soul stared back at us. The hollow feeling at the pit of my stomach sent a wave of emotions through me like a bolt of lightning.

"You made it out, I see," my brother interrupted my musings.

"Barely," I grunted. Against doctors' orders, I decided to get a little air. I ain't gone lie, I feel like shit. I just couldn't be cooped up in the house by myself no more.

"I can't believe you not gone tell me who did this shit to you?"

"Ain't nothing to tell," I said, staring at the flat screen on the wall. I cringed at the score, thinking about the bet I had placed this morning.

"Yea, if you say so. Jade, come give my brother a special on the house." He winked.

The fine chick forced a smile and rolled her eyes all in one. I looked her up and down lustfully, undressing her with my eyes. She caught my gaze and smacked her lips, storming away. I shook the thoughts of what I would do to her out of my mind, trying to stay focused.

It had been months since I'd heard from Desi, and I decided to play shit a little different this time. I planned to just sit back and let her come to me. As planned, she did. She dared to ask me for a divorce. She didn't even have the decency to face me when asking either. I sat in the hospital fighting for my life for almost two months; a punctured lung, internal bleeding, you name it. *"Her selfish ass couldn't even send a postcard."* I chuckled, stroking my chin. I leaned back in my seat and enjoyed the little peep show this Jade girl was giving on the low.

"That you?" I asked my brother, catching her giving him a lil side-eye.

"Nah," he said casually, tossing back his drink.

"Come on, bruh. You hit, didn't you?"

"Get out my shit, Tae," C.J. warned.

"So, you'll let me hit?" I teased, testing him.

"She all yours, playboy," my brother responded.

She must've heard him because she slammed my drink down so hard, I damn near tasted the tension.

"Man, listen, it's something bout a feisty woman. When they get mad, it's so damn attractive and thrilling, like staring a bull in the eyes right before you ride that mutha." I laughed, tossing back the concoction.

"Yea aight, the thrill is fun until that bull tosses yo ass in a shit hole of bullshit," he countered.

In the middle of our convo, this thuggish-ruggish bone-looking ass cat walking in our direction comes.

"The man of the hour has arrived," C.J. hummed.

"What's to it?" He asked with this goofy-ass smile on his face.

"Kane, this is my brother, Dontae. Dontae, this is Kane. The new lion in the den."

Apparently, he thought that last part was funny. "What you mean?" I grimaced, unamused.

"Kane is my new business partner. Weren't you the one that said I needed someone else to help me out around here?"

89

"Yeah, I said that shit, but I ain't think you were just gone bypass me." Chris gave me a blank look. "I'm just saying, though. He ain't family."

"Yeah, yeah," Kane rolled his eyes, placing his intertwined hands on the bar top and leaning forward. "I know that I'm kinda weird and kinda different, but the fact still remains that women love me and real niggaz honor me!" He said, winking at his little fan club in the corner. "I say all that humbly. I'ma Unicorn! I don't need to be family. Besides, sometimes family ain't really family," he said smoothly.

I cleared my throat, unmoved at his little speech.

"Aye C.J., I got some things to tend to, so I'm gone leave y'all to it," he said, looking up from his phone and shaking my brother's hand. He nodded his head upon his exit. "Sometimes, it's all about the company we keep. After all, bad company corrupts good character," he said over his shoulder.

My jaw convulsed in annoyance as my brother walked him out of the club.

"Here is another, and I added a cherry on top just for you," Jade crooned. She pulled the cherry out of the glass and inserted it into her mouth seductively. After a few seconds, she pulled it out, showing me how she'd tied a knot in the stem with her tongue.

"I can always use a little bad company," Jade snickered mischievously, stroking my hand and making my manhood rise.

Kane

Issa vibe

OW I AIN'T NEVA been a people person. I ain't one of them friendly dudes that take to everybody either. But I'm a businessman, and I have no issue with cordiality when necessary. Something about that Dontae cat didn't sit right in my gut. Being in his presence gave me an uncanny feeling along with the darkness in the atmosphere. I had been to club Finesse a few times since me and C. J's last meeting, and I got nothing but good vibes when I was there. It's something inside that cat that made my skin crawl. Getting that call from Desiree gave me enough reason to dip before things became heated because my patience is thin, and my street mentality remains dormant but awakes instinctively.

I walked into my spot, and the smell of a homecooked meal invaded my nostrils immediately. I stepped into the kitchen, and Desiree's back was facing me, her ear glued to the phone. I removed my blazer slowly and folded my arms across my chest while leaning against the wall. I nodded my head in approval as I examined her stature. Although my oversized shirt swallowed her tiny frame, there were parts of her that swallowed my shirt, if you get my drift.

"I just need to get it over with…. he always finds me, Trish…" Her voice was shaky as she carried on her conversation. I wanted to be nosey, but I didn't want to pry. I had a bad habit of taking on other people's problems and making them a project of my own.

"Ahem," I interrupted, causing her to drop her phone in the sink water. "Oh shit, my bad."

She shook her phone off unphased. "You got a real bad habit of sneaking up on folks, I see."

Before I could respond, she turned to face me, and I could have sworn I was just injected by a strong dose of novocaine. I stood there speechless, admiring the fact that she had come a long way from the woman I broke out of the hospital. Her hair was neatly pulled back into a ponytail, and her chocolate skin glowed, complimenting her dimples and brown eyes. To sum it up, she was like a young Naomi Campbell.

I would fuck the shit outta you, gurl, I thought to myself, stroking my chin.

"Excuse me?" She exclaimed with her hands on her hips with a slight smirk.

I couldn't believe I said that out loud. I changed the subject quickly, brushing past her.

"What you doin' in my kitchen, woman?" I asked, peeking into the pots and pans above the fire.

"I just wanted to do something special for you. Just to show a little gratitude for…. you know."

"Nah, you don't owe me nothing, Queen. But I appreciate it. I ain't neva gon' turn down a good meal. Not one that looks and smells as good as this one. But looks can be deceiving," I stated, raising my eyebrow at the chocolate woman that stood in my kitchen.

It's been a few months since Desiree had been camped up in my spot, and today was the first day I looked at her in a whole 'nother light. I hadn't noticed the beauty in this woman.

Maybe that's because I knew how much of a distraction a woman of her caliber could be.

She walked over to me and planted a soft kiss on my cheek. "Well, thank you anyway," she said genuinely.

I grabbed her arm before she could walk away. "What are you running from, Desiree?"

Silence filled the room as her eyes shifted to the marble floors. I grabbed her chin and lifted her eyes to meet mines. "You ain't gotta run no more. You are safe here."

The tears that filled her sultry brown eyes broke me. I hated to see a woman cry. I wondered what it was that had her so broken; I wiped her tears, and she placed her hand on mines. Something about her touch sent a wave of thoughts up and through me.

"What are you afraid of, Kane?" She whispered.

"It's you that's afraid, baby. I'm just here for the ride," I countered, leaning in to kiss her. It was something about this woman that had me hypnotized momentarily.

"Issa vibe," she purred, reading my mind and taking me in with grace.

Two years prior

I awoke to a pounding headache and my rock-hard meat being devoured. The slurps alone made me grow inside her lips. She squirmed in her own juices because giving head alone made her cum. I palmed her ass while I watched her head bob rhythmically. This woman was like a trained assassin to the penis. I could've sworn her tonsils tongue kissed my balls in between grunts and moans; she didn't even come up for air. Just as I was ready to buss, I grabbed the back of her head firmly, turning her on even more. She didn't miss a beat, didn't pull back, didn't spit, nothing.

"Damn, girl!" I smiled while licking my lips.

TY NESHA

I reached over to grab my phone. There were over twenty missed calls.

"*I turned it on silent, so you could rest,*" *Camille said as she used the back of her hands to wipe her mouth, giving me a cunning grin.*

"*Didn't I tell you not to touch my damn phone,*" *I grimaced. She knew exactly what she was doing, and you betta know it ain't have shit to do with me getting no damn rest.*

My sister had been blowing my line down for the past three hours, and I knew she was gone be heated. I jumped to my feet, remembering I had promised her I would watch my niece for her today.

"*You so damn quick to jump to yo' feet for everybody else, but yo' ass can't neva jump when it comes to me, Kane.*"

I ignored her little rant and continued to get dressed while I called my sister back. Her phone was goin' straight to voicemail.

"*Kane!*" *Camille screamed, irking the hell outta me.*

I still kept my cool and grabbed my keys off the dresser. I reached into my wallet and threw a hundred-dollar bill on the bed.

"*For your services,*" *I jolted contemptuously.*

I don't do disrespect, and if I told a woman to respect my shit, that's just what I meant. Camille was not exempt from that. I don't give a damn how good her lips felt wrapped around my manhood. I told her to keep her hands off my phone, and I meant that shit. Females always think a man not wanting a woman to touch his phone meant he was tryna hide something. I'm a grown-ass man; I don't have to hide a damn thing. What Camille and most women fail to realize is, it's about respect. And if you can't respect my privacy, then you have no place in my life. My phone is how I make my money. Insecurity has no place here, and intervening in any way is an automatic dismissal for me; no exceptions.

I gunned my truck through the green light and headed west full speed until I pulled up to Love's job. The commotion outside of the restaurant gave me a weird feeling in my gut. I pushed my way through, attempting to blend in with the small crowd that had gathered around. The paramedics pushed through and toward the horrid screams that haunted my soul, leaving an eerie feeling in the pit of my stomach. I watched as onlookers

94

held their mouths in disbelief. I had seen a lot of shit in my days, faced a lot of adversity, but nothing could prepare me for this day; nothing could prepare me for the devastation that loomed my way.

No More Running

ONCE UPON A TIME, I had a type. I went for a specific kind of man, and Dontae was nothing short of everything I wanted in a man physically and financially. Eventually, I woke up. I realized that in life, there was no such thing as "a type." It all boiled down to character and morality. Kane's whole persona depicted his character effortlessly. He was the total opposite of what I preferred; he was shorter, less fit, his skin color was the exact shade as milk chocolate, a little more chocolate than my taste buds were used to. I examined him as he lay next to me peacefully. I cursed myself for not doing this sooner. I had never made love in such a way. But inside, I felt like I'd betrayed my husband. Although I knew the importance of devotion, in due time, I learned that no matter how loyal I was, how beautiful, in shape, or how well I cooked, none of that mattered to a broken man.

People wonder why I didn't just leave. *Why stay, Desi?* From birth, everyone that mattered to Dontae had abandoned him in some way, shape, or form. So, I figured if I was the total opposite of what he was used to, then whatever it was that had my husband broken, somehow, some way, my love for him could put the pieces back together in due time. But instead, he broke me, leaving me empty with nothing more to give. I gave up on love, and it had become obsolete to me. As much as I wanted to let Kane in, my heart was filled with pain that I

96

couldn't release. I just hoped that he was patient enough to understand.

I bobbed my head to the music as I reminisced in my own little zone. The sound of the phone ringing startled me; I stood over the counter, looking out of the window, wondering who in the hell was calling my phone; only two people had my new number, and I'm sure....

"He… hello", I said through the phone, continuing to cut up the juicy watermelon.

"Desi, is that you?"

"Ma?" I paused, almost slicing off my damn finger. My heart rate sped up as anger and hurt filled me all in one. I turned down the music and swallowed slow, remembering our last encounter.

"He's a dog, Desiree. Can't you see that? I just wanted you to see that dogs have no limitations; they..."

"So, you show me that like this? You show me that my man is a dog by screwing him?"

"What do you want, and how did you get this number?"

"Baby, I need to see you. I heard about what happened and..."

"Heard?"

"I talked to your sister and…" I cursed myself for even calling my sister. She knew damn well I didn't want anyone to find me. I wasn't ready for that, and although Kane made me feel safe every step of the way, something in my soul told me that Dontae wasn't going to let up, no matter how much he cooperated at the moment. His cooperation was sure to have a motive, and until I figured out what that was, I controlled my own movement, how often and how far.

"Desi, baby."

I cringed at how pretentious my mother was. All my life, she tried to control everything and every move, just like a Tae. If you ask me, they deserved one another. Kane was freedom, he was safety, he was...

"Say something, Desi. I just need you to forgive me and tell me where you are. I wanna see your face."

I stared out the window in a daze. Although I missed my mother and my family, I knew deep in my heart that if Tae even thought that there was another man in the picture, it would be a repeat episode.

"*That fool put his hands on you, Desi?*"

"*Nas, calm down, baby. He knows about us; I know he does.*" I panicked, pacing back and forth.

"*And? The fuck that mean? You know damn well I ain't scared of that pussy. As a matter of fact, he owes me a lot of money. I was letting that shit slide on the strength of you, but don't think for a sec...*"

"*Baby, please.*" I sobbed with my hands cupping his face. "*I'm ok, I swear.*"

"*You are not ok, Desiree. This clown thinks he slick. He keeps you locked up like a prisoner because he knows damn well you deserve so much better than him. He knows you are the most beautiful being that ever walked these streets. That's why he puts his hands on you, and I can't respect that shit.*"

"*Please, baby. Let's just go away. We can move somewhere warm. I always hated the cold anyway.*"

"*Oh, we will, baby, we will,*" he said, kissing me on my forehead.

Against my protests, he did what he wanted to do anyways. Three weeks later, I received a phone call that broke my heart in half.

"*Desi baby, I'm sorry. I'm sorry I couldn't be the man you needed me to be. I got in too deep. I love you. Promise me no matter what; you'll make sure you get out before it's too late. I always will be in love with you because you are a good girl. Desi, you don't know much about me and how involved I was in the street life because I kept you away to protect you. But if you live by the sword, you die by the sword. Make sure you keep ya head up, ma. Don't take no disrespect from nobody! And don't feel sorry for yourself. I love you,"* Then he hung up the phone.

That conversation repeated in my head daily. I genuinely miss him, and I can't keep living in fear. Whatever is going to happen will happen. I looked over at Kane, and there was something different that stirred inside his spirit. It's crazy how everything that one man had done to break me, there was another waiting to help piece me back together. I couldn't bring him into my madness. I knew what had to be done, and this time, it had to be done right—no more fear; no more running.

Alexis

Her Trash, My Treasure

"*Girls be getting played and displayed as the goof they are, then wanna be mad at everyone else. Let that hurt go sis.*" My fingers moved quickly as I updated my status, throwing shots at anybody that the shoe fit. Gavin snatched the phone out of my hand and tossed it on the bed.

"What I tell you about that?"

"About what, Gavin?" I asked cleverly as a sly grin spread across my face.

"Yo' ass so damn immature, Lexi. Every time you get mad at me, you go on social media with yo' rants and subliminal posts about a person that has no clue you got a beef with them in the first place."

"Immature?" His words were like alcohol to an open wound. I hated when he did that dumb shit. Any other time it's, "*age ain't nun but a number.*" But as soon as I did something he disapproved of, I was childish and immature.

"Why is it that every time you get mad at your woman, you bring that shit over here trying to downplay me and throw my age in the equation?"

"So, you don't think it's childish to post shit on social media callously, tryna kick shit up?"

100

"You know what, it's my page. I post what the hell I want. You know you got some nerve walking around here like you don't piss the same color as the next dude."

"I don't," he retorted. "My piss is platinum."

"Well, put it in the bottle and sell it, witcha broke ass." Gavin grabbed me by my hair and threw my half-naked body to the bed.

"You got a smart-ass mouth," He hissed, mounting on top of me. Gavin was what some would call a B.O.N; he was my big bear and my protector all in one,

I gazed into his eyes. His face was perfect; even though he was pushing forty, he could pass for his late twenties. His thick dark brows furrowed as we stared at one another. I had seen so much of me in him it was scary. I suddenly felt warm as I imagined him inside me. He gripped my neck forcefully, using his other hand to guide his way inside of me, still holding me with his gaze.

"I love you, Lexi," he whispered.

"I love you more," I moaned, pulling him in closer.

So, now y'all wanna judge me and what I have goin' on with Gavin? She doesn't even want him anymore anyway, and the way I see it, her trash, my treasure. I don't care what nobody thinks or how much y'all twist ya lips and roll ya eyes.

Let me break it down. I really don't like explaining myself, but this time I'll give it to ya straight, no chaser. When I met Gavin, I knew the situation at hand. He kept it all the way solid with me, and I respected that. At that time, he kept me fresh and made sure I ain't need for nothing. In return, I made sure he was satisfied, even exchange. We had an understanding, and as long as he kept it out of my face, I agreed to play nice. It wasn't until one hot ass day in July he came strolling through my place of employment like shit was sweet. Here I was, working on a holiday, and Lord behold, Gavin pulls up, surprising the hell out of me.

"What the hell?" I said, squinting my eyes as if the scenery was going to change. I watched as he walked over to the other side of his ride and opened the door for this sista with short hair and a Fashion-nova romper. I placed Love's baby girl on the sofa in the breakroom and walked over to the window to get a better view. My heart sank as he leaned against her, shoving his tongue down her throat. He looked at her with so much passion, so much affection that I got sick to my stomach. Yea, I knew he had someone, but out of sight, out of mind. It wasn't until that moment I realized that he had never looked at me the way he looked at her. I sauntered in that emotion briefly before I pounced back in my "niggas ain't shit" mode and laughed in disgust at how this bitch had no idea that twenty-four hours prior, his mouth was drowning in my juices.

I looked back, and the little angel was so engrossed in paw patrol. I decided to play along.

"Baby girl. Tee-Tee Lexi will be right back. You stay put, ok?" I said, kissing her on the forehead.

"I'm virsty," she said, tickling my insides.

"Oh, yea? Well, I'll bring you back something to drink if you promise to stay put," I assured her.

She nodded her head up and down with a wide grin. "One more thing! When you grow up, if someone breaks your heart, punch them in the face." Her smile faded, and her big dough eyes grew wider. "No, seriously, punch them in the face and go get some ice cream." I stole that, by the way.

I laughed as I made myself visible just in time. I watched as Love seated them and began to take their order. I made eye contact with Gavin, and his dog ass had the nerve to look past me like I was nothing. I was triggered and made my way over.

"Lexi, this is my friend, Sage." I had heard Love speak of her before, but never Gavin.

"Is she the one that…"

"Convinced me into keeping my baby girl? Yes indeed, she is." Love smiled.

"Nice to finally meet you, Sage," I said with sarcasm only Gavin would understand.

He leaned into her, whispering something into her ear before excusing himself from the table.

I got ready to follow behind him, but Love stopped me in my tracks. "Speaking of my baby girl, could you take Sage to the back? She's going to keep her until my shift is out."

I forced a smile, agreed sourly, and led her to the break room.

"Somebody is here to see you, princess." I sang, but she wasn't there. The couch was empty, and my heart hit the floor.

Damn You to Hell

"Eww, C.J.! Please tell me you did not just fart on my leg."

I pushed myself against her and nibbled on her ear. "That's just a little air girl."

"Air my ass. It stinks." Her nose was scrunched up as she turned her head away from me.

"You so damn disrespectful, my fart don't stink. It smells like *Issey Miyake*."

"I know you lying." We both laughed in unison. It had been four months since Love, and I had begun dating. I had vowed not to get into anything serious, so believe me, when I say I wasn't on that love shit, I was just about making my money. But I couldn't resist this woman. She was like an angel sent by the man himself, handpicked and all with a special delivery.

"Did you tell your brother yet?"

"Huh?"

"You heard me."

"Not yet. I don't know how he's going to feel about…"

"About you interning at the Law Firm?"

"Oh, that," she said with a bit of relief.

"Oh, so yo' ass scared to tell ya brotha how I been knockin' ya back out, huh?" I teased.

"Nah, it ain't that. It's just..."

"Just what?"

"I don't wanna be telling nobody about us, and you can't even put a title on it."

"Aw, here we go..."

"Exactly. You know I been through too much to be repeating the same thing over and over."

"Why you keep saying that like *I'm* the one that put you through the shit? Every time we have this discussion, you bring up ya past like I'm the one that..."

Love rolled her eyes and arose from the bed. I grabbed her arm and pulled her back. I clenched my jaws at the disrespect. One thing I hated was for a person to turn their back on me in the middle of a conversation.

I took a deep breath before continuing on. "Don't walk away from me. Do I walk away from you when you're talking?" I asked calmly.

Silence.

"Oh, you can't talk now?"

"What you want me to say? When I don't want to get smart, I walk away to avoid saying something out of order."

I laughed inwardly before pulling her closer. "You ain't gone say nothing I can't handle. Don't bite yo tongue on my behalf."

She pulled herself up, her stare fixed on me. Her light brown eyes sparkled when she looked at me. I knew just from that she wasn't fronting her moves or how she felt about a brutha. "I know you don't have feelings for me, C.J. You always acting like I'm rushing things, and you don't know how to express yourself."

I laughed to keep from getting upset. It's like women always want some sort of validation on top of what you are already giving them. This is the reason I ain't have time to settle down or get involved. Don't get me wrong, I'm digging Love, and I rock with her the long way. She's beautiful, goal-oriented and her heart is good. It's just, everybody wants to put a time on when to catch feelings or when to put a "title" on it. It's so many things she still doesn't know about me, and I'm not sure she is built for it either.

"Seems there is nothing to talk about. You got all the answers," I said sarcastically.

"I don't have the answers to anything. All I can do is go off what you show me."

"What I show you or what I tell you? It seems to me like the time I spend with you and the affection I show you ain't enough. My actions count for nothin'. You wanna hear something that I'm not sure I'm ready to say. People can't even weather the storm before they wanna put a title on something. We have to be in accord with one another for things to work and last. What happened to building a friendship and letting things happen naturally?"

"I've tried that. I have been there. You say to me I'm making you pay for my past, but when am I going to learn from the same damn patterns, the same lines, and speeches? I'd be a damn fool not to put my foot down one way or the other."

Before I could respond, the sound of my doorbell interrupted me. "I'll be back," I told her as I threw on some sweats and a tee.

"And stop looking at my dick," I teased; she grinned cunningly, raising her eyebrow before I walked out the room. I definitely made a mental note to handle that upon my return.

"Doc," I said in surprise as I welcomed him in. I sensed something was wrong because he never made house visits.

"I've been trying to call you but…."

"Awe, man, my phone was in my bag all night, and I forgot to put it on the charger. What brings you here?" I asked, getting straight to it.

C.J.," Doctor Richards said as he pulled out the chair and placed some papers on the table. He took a brief pause and looked past me.

Love planted a soft kiss on my cheek and said her goodbyes. Though I didn't want her to leave just yet, now was not the time to refute. I returned the gesture and gave her a wink before she walked out of the door.

"Now, where were we?" I asked, turning my attention back to Doctor Richards. Since I was a kid, Doctor Richards has known me, and he was a close friend of the family. The look on his face was a look I had never seen before.

"What's up?" I asked apprehensively.

He removed his glasses and massaged his forehead. "I'm just going to give it to you straight. After meeting with the urologist regarding the test we ran last week, it was bought to my attention that your adrenal glands, the endocrine glands located above each kidney," he said as he pointed to the pictures. "He strongly suspects it could be a pheochromocytoma."

"Pheoch what?" All of this talk was like a whole 'nother language to me. I looked at him, lost and confused. He rested his hand on my shoulder. "I have one of the best surgeons with years of experience in removing these tumors on board."

"Surgeons?"

Doctor Richards sighed, "The urologist's diagnosis has been confirmed, and they have convened a team of physicians to plot a course of action for you."

"So, I gotta have a surgery?" I said, asking the obvious.

"I don't know how else to say this, but C.J...."

The light tap at the door put our conversation on pause, confusing the hell outta me. Being that I ain't had this many visitors in ages, and I don't do pop-ups. Hell, I don't even give out my address.

I opened the door, and Satan himself stared me in my face.

"I see you still telling folk I'm dead."

Time had stood still, and my world began to spin momentarily. "I visit your grave every week," I countered furiously.

"Well, I see you still stubborn as the day you left, boy."

I couldn't believe this shit. The nerve of him to show his face at my doorstep.

"Damn you to hell, old man," I spat viciously.

"So, that's how you speak to your father?"

"Father?" I chuckled and sucked my teeth. "I have no father. In my mind, he's dead, and he forever will be." I spat before closing the door in his face.

"Now, where were we?" Doctor Richards had a look of disbelief on his face. He shook his head to the side before rising from his seat. He walked over to me and looked me in my eyes.

"You have cancer, C.J., and it's spreading pretty fast." Was the last thing I heard before my world shattered in a split second.

Sage

Tears of Confliction

"*Arggggggghhhh!*" *I screamed as the sweat beads rolled down my forehead.*

"*Push, girl, we almost there!*" *My mother screamed in my ear.*

It felt like my head was going to explode; I was pushing so hard. "I'm tryin'." I grunted in between breaths.

"*Try harder!*" *My mother spat.*

"*Ma'am, she is under enough pressure, and we need to keep her calm if we want this labor to be successful....*"

"*Listen,*" *My mother hissed, cutting the doctor off. "Don't tell me how to speak to my child, and for all its worth, I don't care about a successful nothing. Her fast ass aint have no business spreading her legs and getting pregnant no how.*"

Mama and I ain't never really get along much after my daddy left, and I feel like the only reason she even let me stay with her was to use me as a pawn to punish him. I could never understand why she hated me so much, aside from the fact that I was the spitting image of him. I always did what she asked me to do; I didn't talk back; I helped her out around the house as much as I could. No matter what I did, she was never satisfied. I always promised myself when I had my baby, I don't care how the father and I end up; I will never make her pay for that.

109

I gave it one final push. "I see the head." The kind nurse said, giving me a sincere smile.

"You can do it; you're doing great," she continued. All the cheers I'd wish were from the mouth of my mother. Instead, her nasty ways made me push even harder to keep from hearing her rant about me not having any business getting pregnant, no how.

"It's a girl!" The nurse chirped. My mother stormed out of the room, and moments later, the most saintly cries graced my ears, sending a force of chills through my body.

"Can I hold her?" I asked timidly as they cleaned her and swaddled her body into the blanket.

"Of course, you can," the nurse said as she placed her into my arms carefully.

I wrapped my arms around her and examined her little body. Counting all five fingers and toes. Her dark curly hair stuck to her forehead. I pulled it back from her face, and she had the most unique birth mark beneath her hairline.

"My baby girl," I exhaled. "My baby girl."

"Sage, do you hear me talking to you?" Gavin's baritone voice broke my thoughts.

"I heard you, baby. I was just thinking how proud of you I am. I told you, you wouldn't stay down long. Just a little faith and patience," I assured him, wrapping my arms around his neck.

Gavin put his forehead against mines and planted a soft kiss against mines.

"I know I ain't been treating you right, Sage, and you been so damn good to me, girl." Those words sent a rush of flutters through me. He continued, and I listened gracefully, appreciating every word. This was the man I fell in love with. This was the man that would do anything in his power to show me that he was willing to go to the moon and back to see me smile, and I would do the same for him. Guilt plagued my mentality as I thought about Dom. I was conflicted between the love I held for Gavin and the void Dom had begun to fill. I could feel Gavin's cell vibrate in his jeans. I let out an exasperated breath before I attempted to pull away.

"Where you goin'?" He asked, pulling me back in.

"Don't you gotta get that?"

"Nah, it can wait."

Gavin never shoo'ed off his phone without even looking at it. Even if he'd decline the call, he would check it first. After all these years, his patterns, his games, and everything about him had become predictable. After all these years, I was too naïve and afraid to walk away and start over.

"I have to tell you something," I admitted apprehensively. He began to kiss my neck as he cornered me against the wall, ignoring my plea. My special place pulsated the same rhythm in which my heart would beat. It had been so long that he and I had slept together; it had been so long since I had an orgasm of any sort, for that matter. The most I had done with Dominick was kiss and dry hump like two damn teenagers. Gavin's lips and hands worked their way down my body as he pulled my pants down. He lifted me off my feet and carried me over to the sofa while letting his tongue enter my sugar bowl. I gyrated my hips as I wrapped my legs around his neck and held his head steadily.

He knew exactly what to do to make me melt and turn putty right into his mouth. His tongue reached depts of me that I hadn't even discovered. Just as I was ready to release to quench his thirst, he palmed my ass and held me tightly while he sucked all of my juices, sending an explosion throughout my body effortlessly.

He laid my body down on the couch and pulled me into him.

"Gavin…I…"

"Marry me," he whispered, pulling a ring out of his pocket.

My eyes widened at the words I'd been longing to hear for so long.

"Yes," the word escaped my mouth without thought as he placed the 14 carats, princess cut, white gold ring on my finger.

My hand clasped my mouth as the tears ran down my face. But little did he know, these were not tears of joy. These were tears of confliction. Two men had proposed to me, and I said yes to them both.

I Choose Me

I SIFTED THROUGH THE sales rack of Neiman Marcus. It'd been so long since I've had a date that I couldn't even remember what it felt like. I was used to Dontae showering me with gifts and money, but us going out was rare, being that I had a new bruise every other week. I watched as the lady pushed her child in the stroller and looked through racks of clothes. She was in her element, and her beauty stood amongst a sea of people. I remained incognito as I worked to muster up enough nerves to approach her. My body floated towards her against my own will; she looked so worn out and drained. The child in the stroller pulled down clothes from the racks as she stood in a daze. I could feel her energy begin to interweave into mines. She was a replica of who I used to be; she was so….

"Excuse me, miss. May I help you?" One of the sales clerks sang livelily.

"Uh, yes, this doesn't have a price, and I was wondering if…"

"Desi? Desiree Williams?" She yelped, almost blowing my cover.

I removed my oversized Ray Bands from my face and pursed my lips together, forcing a smile.

113

"Oh my goodness, it is you!" She exclaimed, pulling me in for a hug.

"It's been so long. I haven't seen you since senior year."

Confusion filled my face as I tried to remember who the girl was. Since I didn't really talk to many girls in high school, I couldn't put together who....

"Porsha Greene?" I hissed. My nostrils flared as I tried to maintain my composure while looking the once beautiful bombshell up and down in disgust. Porsha Greene was the most popular girl in high school. She was every guys' dream girl with her porn star breasts and flawless everything. Head to toe, she was the shit, ok. But what I couldn't understand was how in the hell she went from Tyra Banks to Precious in a matter of years. This chick standing in front of me made my head spin as I thought back to the last day we crossed paths.

"It's the last week of school Desi, and you still acting like a prude," my best friend, Charlie, whined in my ear as we walked home from the school.

"Listen, I gotta make sure I finish strong; otherwise, moms not going to let me go for the internship at the modeling agency this summer."

Even at seventeen, my moms had a tight grip around my neck. Her rules were intolerable, and being that I was starting to come out of my shell and blossom, it didn't seem like she was going to loosen the leash anytime soon. Doing this internship was my only out, and I wasn't doing anything to mess that up.

Just as Charlie and I turned on my block, we spotted Brian and some of his homies shooting dice on the stoop.

"Desi!" Brian called out, pulling me by my arm. I had the biggest crush on Brian all the way back from the sixth grade, and though our mothers were best friends, he never looked at me twice until my senior year. By then, he was already stamped by Porsha herself, and I ain't want no problems.

"What's up, Brian?" I said nonchalantly, pulling away from him.

"You looking real good today," he flirted, making my heart do cartwheels.

Before I could respond, I spotted Porsha and her puppets coming from the opposite direction. Not wanting any beef, I thanked him and created a space in between us.

"Where you goin'?" He asked, pullin' me back, exposing his dimple.

Before I knew it, I felt a solid grip on my hair and blows coming from every direction. Falling to the ground, I noticed Charlie throwing blows. Her hands were quick, but we were clearly outnumbered. I covered my face and head, shielding myself from the kicks and impacts, while everyone gathered around, heckling at us.

Porsha stooped down before me, giving me a menacing glare. "Bitch, yo black ass would never have a chance in hell with my man, you heard me." I could feel the blood dripping from my head as it leaked into my eyes. I winced, looking up at who was supposed to be my childhood friend take the side of this diabolical bully. I forced my way up and pulled Charlie up with me before dusting myself off. I, for one, was tired of these bitches trying to make my life a living hell and the only way around it was....

"So, you mad, Porsha? For what? Because you know yo' man digging the hell outta my 'black ass', huh? Well, I'll let you in on a little secret. His ass been pissin' in the bed since he was five. Don't nobody want yo' pissy ass boy toy. Face it. All this animosity stems from you being intimidated by this chocolate ass girl. You mad because yo' man wants me to melt in his mouth, so I can grace him with some new flavor, ain't you?" My heart raced as the slew of protests escaped my mouth. I knew I was asking for more trouble, and you better believe they beat my ass after I was done, but it was one of the most liberating moments of my life, and I wouldn't change it if I could.

"Listen, I want to apologize for...."

I put my hand up, interrupting her. "It's all good, Porsha. No apology needed," I said, looking in the other direction.

"Would you excuse me? I have something I need to take care of." I walked off, leaving her to wallow in thought, leaving my fragrance lingering in the air.

"He's handsome," I said, startling the young lady.

"Oh, thank you," she said, avoiding eye contact.

"He's beating the living daylights out of you, isn't he?"

"I don't know what you are talking about." She fidgeted.

"It doesn't stop! It only gets worse," I continued. "What's his name?"

She paused before shifting her eyes up to mines.

"Dontae Junior," She mumbled. "He's three years old." She added as a cascade of tears streamed down her cheeks.

"I…I'm sorry…I…"

"No, baby, I'm sorry. My hell is now yours, and this is what you wanted, baby; now he's all yours. I spent years waiting on him to change and make things right. I chose to accept his flaws and everything that came with him, even when he thought I didn't know," I said, looking down at the spitting image of Dontae. "My decision-making skills ain't been too good in my days. I made my choice to stay, but now, now he's your problem. See, today I choose me, and I'd have to admit, everything is unfolding as it should. That baby needs his mama alive and well. Looks like you got your own choices to make, dear." I turned away and left her in her thoughts. I rubbed my protruding belly, smiled, and thanked God for change.

All I See Is You

I DROVE IN CIRCLES, forgetting where I was headed, bobbing my head to *Medicine* by that one chick Queen Naija. I mouthed the words to the song, let down my windows, and let the cool breeze kiss my skin. *"If it feels too good to be true, it usually is."* The words of my metaphorical brother popped into my head. I left C. J's place with my head in a frenzy. I remained conflicted with our conversation, and I bounced back and forth like a ping pong ball; if it would be a smart thing for me to do to carry on this "thing" without clarity. I mean. I don't understand why he would waste my time no how.

Amid my thoughts, a smile spread across my face as my phone pinged a notification that played a tune to the one person that composed its own melody deep down in my soul. Just like that, I was sucked into his charm. See, C.J. was one of them smooth-talking negros. You know the ones that will talk shit and sell you the water you already have possession of. I loved the way he made me feel; yet, I despise the fact that a man can have such power over a woman's emotions. Like, they can come in, sweep you off your feet, carry you into la-la land, and have you smiling ear to ear glowing. And all of a sudden, just like that, they can snatch the rug from beneath you and take you right back to the hell they found you in. Even though

117

the pain was unbearable at times, I wondered if it was worth it; one more shot could do some severe damage and throw me so far overboard that I may not return.

I pulled up to the abandoned building, blindsided by the pungent aroma of piss and garbage assaulting my nostrils. I rolled my windows up in disgust, hoping the smell didn't seep into my ride. I looked around at my old neighborhood. "The wild hunnids" they called it. I couldn't believe I grew up in these streets. My brother tried his hardest to shield me from this world, but he had no idea that even though he moved us into the suburbs the first chance he got, I still found my way back until the last day I stepped foot on this block.

"Tia, you already know Kane is not goin' for that, so I don't even know why you're asking."

My best friend, Tia, smacked her lips and put her hands on her hips. "That's why we ain't gone tell 'em," she stressed. "Cause if you go down, I go down. You know Kane ain't got no problem putting a foot up both of our asses," she said, pulling the string for the next stop.

"Exactly, which is the reason why we shouldn't be doin' this," I protested. "I'm taking the next bus back, Tia. So, if what you got to do gone take longer than that next go-round, then...."

"Just c'mon," she said, tugging on my shirt. Tia already knew I was not gone leave her. Our moms were best friends, and Tia and I were connected at the hip since birth. Even though we moved away, Tia and I made sure we got together every time I came to visit my mom.

No sooner than we stepped off the bus, there were dudes everywhere hooping and hollering at us and our fully developed fifteen-year-old bodies.

Tia rocked a red crop top with a pair of oversized denim overalls and some all-white Adidas. Her hair was in a silky wrap, and it covered one eye just like that singer Aaliyah. Her deep dimples penetrated every time she spoke. She was only 5'1, but her body made up for her size, no doubt. Her large name chain swerved side to side as she pulled me across traffic and over to a group of boys I'd never seen before.

118

"Yo' Tia! Who yo' friend?" One of the boys asked with a weird grin on his face.

"Mouse, this my girl, Love. Love, this is Mouse, Meechie, Puma and-"

"And Maurice." One of the boys interjected, introducing himself.

"Maurice, you so damn extra," Tia said, rolling her eyes.

"Love is my sista. We got the same dad," She lied. "She moved to Homewood our eighth-grade year, so she ain't too familiar with the new neighborhood crew." Tia chuckled.

I looked down at my watch apprehensively. Two buses had already passed us by, and there was an eerie feeling lingering in the air.

"You got somewhere you need to be, Love?" Maurice asked, putting his arm around my shoulder.

"Tia," I hissed through clenched teeth, giving her a side-eye, letting her know it was time to bounce.

"Ok, girl, dang," she squealed as she grabbed the joint from one of the boys passing in rotation.

"Here, take a hit. Relax," she said, passing me the weed. I looked around, and all eyes were on me. I put the joint to my lips and inhaled deeply. It burned so bad, I started coughing something crazy. They all laughed and heckled as I took another pull, trying to redeem myself.

"You got them baby lungs," Maurice said as he took the weed out of my hand and put it to his lips.

I dropped my head in embarrassment. "That's all good; I got you," he said, lifting my head up with his finger. "Open your mouth," he said charmingly.

"What?"

"Just do it."

I turned my head for a sec and noticed Tia all huddled up in the corner with the Mouse boy,

"I'm gone give you a shotgun." He nodded.

"I don't want no gun..."

"Girl, not a real gun. Just open your mouth. I'm gone blow the smoke in, and you gone inhale it. Slow though and swallow it. Then exhale it through your nose."

I did as he instructed as he blew a gust of smoke into my mouth. He was so close, I thought he was gonna...

"Ewwwww," I said, pushing him away and wiping my lips.

"I had to." He raised his hands in surrender and laughed.

I gave him a mean mug, dug the heel of my shoe into the concrete, and spun around in Tia's direction. The screeching tires pierced my ears, and the sound of gunshots rang out; everybody scattered as I stood froze.

"Come on, girl!" Maurice screamed, snatching me behind the building.

I watched in terror as I watched body after body drop as my best friend ran in my direction. Her body jolted as one bullet ripped through her petite frame.

"Ahhhhh!" She shrieked in pain, trying to keep moving. I screamed in horror as I tried to run out to her, but the boy held me tightly and wrapped his hand around my mouth. One final shot rang out as the bullet went straight into Tia's head as she fell motionlessly.

A solemn tear fell down my cheek as I placed the flowers against the building. The mural of the many lives lost in Chi-town was growing by the minute. Each life taken, left a hollowness in the lives of those they left behind. I zoned in; her face stood out amongst the others.

"All I see is you," I whispered as I kissed my fingers and placed them on her red lips.

My Final Goodbye

"C.J., you haven't touched your food since I sat it on the table. As much as you eat, I know something's not right." Like a little kid, I picked apart my food, stuck in my thoughts. I was mind-boggled by the series of events that hit me back to back.

"I got a lot on my mind, Love. Just tryna sort things out is all."

"Is it me? Did I do something?" She asked, face all twisted up. I grabbed her hand and pulled her in, sitting her on my lap.

"Of course not." I smiled. "I got a lot of business meetings, and I gotta get some things squared away with the Lion's Den."

"Oh really? So, tell me this… if you are the lion of the den, what does that make me?" She asked with a smirk spread across her face.

"That makes you, my Lioness," I assured her, making her blush.

Love is a damn good woman, and any man in their right mind would be foolish not to make her their one and only. Women like her were hard to come by. On my end, there were many reasons why I couldn't give her a clear-cut answer; too many things at this moment. I hadn't even told her the real

121

reason for me being in the picture. I didn't know-how. I had it all planned out. But in life, your plans and the reality of how things pan out are two totally different effects. Things weren't supposed to get this far, and I don't know how the hell I'm going to charm my way out of this one.

In too deep, I don't even know where to begin. On top of that, it was never my intention to get serious with any woman after what went down between my ex-wife and me. I was blindsided by how things went left. Out the blue came Love, and we began to grow a bond and build. I know this will not end well, and something in my gut tells me there is no such thing as a happy ending in this story. I kissed Love on the forehead and assured her that she was not the problem. I was sure that the skeletons in my closet were too raw for a woman as delicate as Love Wright. A man of my caliber did not deserve a woman so genuine and kind. I had done too many things and hurt too many people, including her. I just needed a little time.

As I planned for my father's funeral, the real funeral this time, I thought back to the day he paid me a visit. A gut-wrenching pain filled my stomach, making me nauseous.

"So, you expect me to feel bad about your ailing wife?" I laughed ragefully.

"She is sick, and she asked for me to get everyone together. She wanted to…"

"Wanted to what?" I asked mockingly.

My father let out an exasperating breath before lighting his cigar. "Why do you hate me so much, son? After all, I have done for you. I made sure you never needed for anything. I gave you the world, and you gave me hell. I gave you life, and you preyed on my death. Why son? What have I done so bad that you must turn your back on me?"

I stroked my chin and let his statement resonate.

122

"You need to tell him the truth. Tell him and mend the relationship with your father. Your pain is the real cancer in your life, and we both know it." Dr. Richards' words rang in my head as I listened to my father try to plead his case. I couldn't believe this man was sitting in my face playing the victim. He figured that money and material things could buy amnesia, but some things you can't forget or ignore.

"The fact that you want me to forget is beyond me. You chose to turn your head to the real issues. See, being a pretender is not my forte; that's all you," I hissed. "Tell me, 'father' how could you not know what was happening in your own home?" I asked, trying to maintain my composure. I had tried to bury the memories, tried to put all of the thoughts behind me, and pretend that they had never happened. But the fact remained, every bit of it had happened, and I had to live with it every day of my life until the day I decided to bury my father in my head and forget I had ever had one.

"I have no idea what you're talking about, C.J.," my father countered, blowing a gust of smoke in the air.

I banged my fist against the wall ragefully. My father jumped, dropping his cigar into his lap.

"Stop lying, old man!" I screamed. The base in my voice resounded against the hollow walls. I could feel a cascade of tears streaming down my face. "I needed you, I needed you to believe me, but you chose her over your son," I sobbed, beating against the wall in between words. "How could you not know that your wife was molesting your son every night for ten years. She took.... she took my virginity. She took away my..."

"Man up, C.J.! You act like you afraid of a little vagina? She was breaking you in. You act as if you didn't like it. You didn't participate...Like you..." In between his statement, there was a short pause. I looked over at my father, gripping his chest in pain as he fell to the floor. I watched contently as he gasped in between breaths. I walked over to him and kneeled to his side...

"Get brave old man! You afraid of a little chest compression? Feels like your heart is 'bout to pop out ya chest, and the world is closing in on you, don't it?"

"Wha… what did you do?" He gasped.

"Nothing, I didn't do nothing," I whispered. "You did…I just came to say my final goodbyes. Your grave awaits you. Don't worry, your dear wife will be joining you soon."

I held tight to the letter attached to my father's will. My father had subsequently left Dontae less than half of the $800,000.00 in his estate. Everything else was left to me; nothing left to his wife. Baffled by the news, the money didn't move me. However, "the letter" made things more complicated than one could ever imagine. My father knew about his first born after all, amongst other things. The irony is, it took his death and a well-written letter of clarity to confirm we were more alike than I would ever envision. Throwing a monkey wrench in the game and me putting a rush on karma made me next in line. But not before I put the ultimate touch on one final thing by righting one wrong before I left this earth. Time is ticking, and we all know it waits for no one.

A Nightmare Worth Living

"A baby? What? I can't believe it. My big brother is having a baby!" Love screamed in excitement.

"That's right, sis, you gone be an auntie."

"Wait, who is the mom, Kane? How you gone have a baby, and I don't even know the mama?" She asked with her hands on her hip.

"I know. It all happened so fast, but I told her I had someone special I wanted her to meet, and I'll leave the rest up to you. Play nice."

"Ha! As much hell, as you have caused my exes, now you want me to play nice. Game on my brother, game on." She teased, rubbing her hands together.

My sister was the first person I'd told about the baby. There weren't too many things I kept under wraps when it came to her. I looked at her proudly as she paced back and forth, throwing out baby names and making plans to throw a baby shower and so forth. I think I lost her at the gender reveal thing. I sure as hell wasn't trying to be doin' too much extra. She already knew I was a simple man and an introvert. I preferred to remain that way as much as possible.

125

Love reminded me so much of our mother. She was the spitting image of her, and I wished that she was here to see how much her timid little girl had transformed into the woman she had hoped she'd be. After our father passed away from a diabetic stroke, our mother had lost her mind and started dating a heroin dealer. We lost her to him. Big Mike was his name. Our mother had so much potential, but potential ain't shit when you got the wrong company on yo side. He had got my mother so hooked on that shit that we didn't even know who she was half the time. Love would try to save her. She would hide the dope, throw out the needles, and she even called herself calculating a plan that would send Big Mike away for a long time; it didn't work. Yet and still, our mother was too far gone. They found her in the alley on Love's seventeen birthday with a needle dangling from her arm and naked. Six months later, they found Big Mike in the same alley shot up and burnt beyond recognition. The only way they were able to identify him was by his bottom gold grill. His murder remained a mystery, one that hasn't been solved to this day.

I had made so many mistakes that I felt like a complete disappointment to my baby sister. I paid for that every time I lived to open my eyes another day. Before I left town, I decided to entomb one of the darkest secrets, a secret that would cost me, my sister, forever.

"Kane! I just got word them boys posted up on the block like shit sweet."

I sat at the kitchen table, counting the money made from our last drop. We had taken a significant loss after one of the trap houses had been hit, and my homie Bo D. got whacked. I had made a call to lay low for a few months to get my sister out of the neighborhood and somewhere safe. Once the war began, bodies dropped everywhere, and the shit went on forever. I leaned back into my seat and stroked my chin, thinking of a play.

"Give it a few more days, Lil Money. We will catch 'em slippin' again. Make 'em think shit sweet for now."

"Man Kane, what the hell we waiting on? We know where they at right now. When have you ever been one to let a simp think shit was sweet? You getting soft." Adonis hissed.

I gathered myself and took a deep breath while massaging the bridge of my nose. Adonis knew better than to test me, and I really ain't have time for his impulsive ass shenanigans, but part of me knew he was right. This was the perfect time to slide on them 112 pussy's. The only thing holding me up was that my mom was scattering up and through there every now and again. Against my better judgment, I decided to handle things my way. Any other time, I would make the call and send a message. But for my homeboy, I chose to pay them a visit personally.

Three cars deep, we loaded up and headed to the Southside to make a statement.

Behind the tent, I could see them clowns posted up just like Adonis said. I placed the red bandana around my face and rolled my window down slowly. I stuck my A-k 47 out the window and sprayed the whole block. Bodies dropped, and screams filled the air, but it was already too late; war was declared.

A few hours after the incident, I walked into my spot, and Love was sitting on the couch covered in blood. I ran over to her in fear that they had struck back. Tears filled her eyes.

"I'm sorry. I know you told me not to go back there, but it was only for a second, Kane." Confusion filled me as she continued to explain in between sobs and gasping for air.

"Love, what happened? Where did you go, Love?" Just as she opened her mouth, I saw the chain in her hand. The same chain that glistened into my shades earlier today.

"They killed Tia, Kane. She's gone."

That was the day I realized that my sister could have easily been the one in the casket. Tia was like my baby sis too and when she died, so did a piece of me. Especially knowing that I had pulled the trigger. A bullet ain't never had no name on it, and once you pulled that trigger, there was no turning back.

TY NESHA

Love finding out would be my worst nightmare, which made
keeping the secret a nightmare worth living.

The Great Pretender

"So, have you decided what you wanna name her yet?" Sage sat at the edge of the bed, rocking my baby girl to sleep.

"No. I figure I'd leave that up to...."

I could feel the tension in the air as Sage took a deep breath before standing.

"Would you like to hold her?" She more so protested, placing her into my arms.

"Let me tell you a story, Love," she said as she swaddled the baby girl in the blanket. "No one knows this story, not even Gavin," she continued, raising her eyebrows. "I was just knocking on fifteen when I had my daughter. My mom, she sent me away." She paused, waving her hands dismissively. "By the time I gave birth, they had me so damn doped up, I didn't have a clue what was goin' on. I should've known something was up when my mother's tune changed, and all of a sudden, she was this supportive woman that I had never seen before." She chuckled. "Anyways, they had taken my baby girl out of my arms and told me I needed to fill out the paperwork for the birth certificate. Who would have known that I was signing over my rights as a mother? I had given my baby up for adoption, and that haunts me every day. All I have to remember is that one moment that I held her in my arms, that one moment when she gripped

*my finger with her tiny hands." The tears fell from her eyes as I looked
into the eyes of my baby girl.*

"I don't know how I can do this on my own with law school and..."

*"And you are not on your own. I will be there with you every step of
the way. This baby..." she said, stroking her forehead. "She is a blessing.
She gave me hope to keep looking for my baby girl, and one day, I will
find her Love. And I have you to thank for that. I will never forget her
face and the birthmark...it was...."*

I shook my head, trying to push the thoughts out of my
mind. It's been almost two years since my life was flipped
upside down; me and anxiety have been together ever since. It
tickles me when folk walks around bragging about having
Anxiety and Depression or being Bipolar. They think it's all
fun and games until you're staying up all night because you
can't stop yourself from overthinking. Wanting to cry and not
even knowing why. Feeling alone, no matter how many people
you surround yourself with or how about the random and
extreme mood changes. What makes having this shit even
more challenging is not wanting to tell people because you
think they won't understand you and begin to view you in
another light. I'm in and out, up and down, hot and cold; this
is no joke. Not being able to control your own mind and
emotions ain't shit to play with. It was a miracle that I could
push through law school and pass the bar before I even
graduated.

"How the hell did you become a Lawyer without a law degree?" Kane's
question made me chuckle. He'd never heard of anyone
conquering what seemed to be impossible in his eyes.

Before moving back to Chicago, I met a big-time attorney
in Cali. He needed help, and I needed a job. He assured me
that with my experience, his training, and hard work, I could
pass the bar without even having to step foot into a school. So,
there I was, for five years, serving as an apprentice receiving
on-the-job training under his guidance. We had gotten serious,
and I had gotten pregnant, only to discover he wasn't available.

After two years of being with this man, we had never solidified anything, and every time the subject came up, he let me know how a title would change nothing and how labels didn't guarantee faithfulness.

"Do you know how many miserable people are in relationships? That doesn't make things perfect. What we have is special, and in due time, things will just flow and happen naturally."

I listened to that garbage for so long until the day I gave him the pregnancy test. We had planned to start a new life together, and he fed me that shit for another eight months. We had finally gotten a place together, and that's when I got a visit, a visit from his "wife." How in the hell did I work under him for so many years and not know that he was married? Simple, the same lies he fed to me, he had fed her sweeter lies. His busy days and long nights at work were all a part of his facade. And how convenient was it that his wife lived in a whole 'nother town and was just as much of a workaholic as he claimed to be? All this time, he wanted me to trust his actions when all along he was just a great pretender.

That was the day I learned that people can be whoever you want them to be as long as they are getting what they need out of the deal. I had turned a blind eye to the obvious. His actions and his words were never going to align because he was already unavailable. I was knocked up by a married man and left with a bitter taste in my mouth for a very long time. I didn't feel right with my unofficial ex being able to remind me how I wouldn't be where I was if it wasn't for his lying ass. Heading back home seemed to be the best choice, and after getting it wrong so many times, it was finally beginning to look up in all areas. Graduating with honors, those alphabets behind my name meant more to me than taking the easy route. On the other end, had it not been for C.J., I don't know where I would have found the strength to believe in love again. He had shown me the reason why none of my other relationships had lasted, and I appreciated him for that.

I walked into Club Finesse with a surprise that was going to blow C.J.'s wig back. After singing at the club, I had finally begun recording in the studio in my free time. Being a lawyer meant paying the bills, but it's not my dream; it was my mother's. Singing was and always has been my passion; it came naturally. I recorded a whole album right under his nose, and today he would be the first to hear it while I entertain him and rock his boat all at the same damn time.

"Hey, Love!" Tess, one of the bartenders sang.

"Hey mama. Chris in the back?"

"I think so. Just go on back, girl. You know you ain't gotta ask," she chuckled.

I hadn't even turned the corner good before I heard Jade chuckling down the hall. That bitch couldn't stand me for whatever reason, and I really didn't give a damn. Before I could reach the door to his office, my heart sank like the titanic. I stared into the glass window and watched Jade straddled over him with her tongue down his throat.

Practice Makes Perfect

MY HANDS WENT ACROSS her face before I could even think about my actions. I knew better than to put my hands on a woman, but Jade caught me off guard, and she tested me every chance she got.

"What is your problem, C.J.? I…"

"Get out my office, man," I grimaced, more pissed at myself.

"I figured you'd be happy." She winced, struggling to her feet. Her lips twitched like she may cry.

"Happy about what, Jade? That after I gave you money for an abortion, you waited four months to tell me you decided to keep a baby that you don't even know who it belongs to?"

"I just found out. I wasn't sure if it was yours, so I decided to wait until my doctor's appointment to find out how far along I was and…"

"And I ain't tryna have no baby with you," I countered. "A doctor's appointment doesn't guarantee my paternity either. I damn sure ain't tryna find out, though."

Jade looked at me like I was the scum of the earth. I don't even know how the hell she managed to be so far along and hide that shit so well, all while working right under my nose.

"I'll see you in court. Thanks for the advance, though. My daughter and I will be cool. Just keep them checks rolling in," she retorted before slamming the door behind her.

"Fuck!" I spat, knocking the papers off my desk.

It's funny to me how this "my body, my right" bullshit worked. Don't get me wrong, I made my choice, I played my part, and I knew better than to stick my dick in this woman without no rubber even though she told me she couldn't get pregnant. I just don't get how a woman can choose to kill my seed even if I wanted it; I was willing to play my part and be the standup father every child deserves or keep my seed. Even if I wasn't ready, made a mistake, a bad choice, or just wasn't trying to go through the hell a bitch like Jade would put me through for the rest of my life. A woman makes a mistake, she has an option, but a brotha gets whatever the woman decided to dish out and will go to jail if he opts out. After all the shit I had went through this week, I don't know how shit could get worse.

"That was a pretty intense scene," Love's voice calmed me and made me uneasy all in one.

I took a breath, bracing myself at her sight. "Love, it's not..."

"Not what I think? I know," she chuckled sarcastically, waving her hand.

"I always hated those movies where the woman runs off before she could get the full story." She grinned artfully. I pulled her in and kissed her lips sensually; for a brief moment, everything else was irrelevant.

"That means you..."

"Know that she's pregnant? I knew that months ago. You see her nose? If that ain't the nose of a pregnant woman, then I don't know what is." She laughed.

"I guess I never got that. I wasn't checkin' for her nose or nothing else for that matter. Love, if that's my baby, I'm gone give her what she wants, and I'm signing over my rights."

"What? You can't do that, C.J., and I would be less of a woman if I stood by that," She emphasized.

"Do you know how much drama she will bring? She doesn't want nothing but the money anyways."

She rolled her eyes. "I don't care, C.J. Right is right, and it's too many young girls out here fatherless. That shit can mess up a girl's whole life. I should know," she said, lowering her voice.

Not wanting to discuss this any further, knowing I wasn't goin' to be changing my outlook any time soon, I stroked her hand and gave her a seductive stare.

"I'm all the daddy you need, girl," I said smoothly, pulling her shirt over her head.

"How did I not meet you sooner?" She panted while I sat her on my desk. Her auburn hair was placed in a neat bun. Her eyes sparkled when she looked in mines; everything about them serenaded me.

I leaned in closer and pulled her pants down with ease. "I gave you time to practice. After all, practice makes perfect," I whispered before sliding inside her. She let out a soft moan as she clutched me tightly, taking me in like a champ.

I saw her lips move, but her words were muted by the hand of a mad woman bringing a high heel down to my head. I had become immune to the pain, yet my soul cried as the warm blood stained my clothing while

seeping through my fingers. The sound of blood leaking from my skull echoed through the walls in my head as they kissed the tile beneath me. Her eyes were empty as they burned holes through my 12-year-old body. She was not my mother. She was nothing more than the wife of my father. None other than a woman that used every opportunity to put the "step" in stepmother to use by using her position to torment, abuse, and mistreat my mother's only Son.

A hand on my shoulder brought me back from my dream. I could barely keep my eyes open as I gasped for air. I cracked open my eyes, a smile struggling to form despite the pain as her beautiful face filled my vision. She was the reason I was still alive. The reason I had found the strength to keep on and through it all, I hadn't been completely honest with her. After refusing chemo, Dr. Richards informed me that cancer had spread. Yet and still, I refused to allow them to put me through the same misery they had placed on my mother. After undergoing all that bullshit, she still ended up dying, leaving me with images of her that plagued me constantly.

I looked over at the one woman that was willing to step in the ring and go toe to toe with any battle I faced. But I couldn't let that happen. I couldn't let my shit become her burden.

I had to figure out a way out of this.

"Love, I need to tell you something," I professed, stroking her hand gently.

"What's up, baby?" She smiled. My phone pinged, and I went to silence it, but it was a message from Dom.

"I know it took me forever to get back to you, but I got the results. Meet me at the club in an hr."

Sage

Misery Loves Company

"It's always a "low-key" hater pressed that they are doing so much better in this world than you! See, I'm happy with the way things are going on in my life. I wish others would do the same and stop being a hater. It doesn't look good."

Love handed me a cup of Patron and plopped down on the pillow beneath me. I took a sip and placed it on the coffee table.

"Sage, why do you always think Lexi hates on you? Why can't she be inspired or…"

"Cut the shit, Love," I hissed as I separated the hair and placed it into her hand. "I only became friends with her on the strength of you. You and I both know I don't do friends. I love her, I really do. I just think her delivery is whack, and the subliminal shit she does shows."

"Maybe it's not about you, though. Do you know how many people fit the criteria of the stuff she is speaking about? Hell, we know Lexi got a smart mouth, but we also know deep inside her heart is pure." Her tinder-headed ass flinched as she tried to play mediator.

137

I heard what Love was saying, and I get it; I really do. I ain't one to get mad at a person being honest with me, and most of the time, I keep my issues to myself, especially if I ain't plan on changing it no time soon. Alexis is dope, don't get me wrong. I know she's young, and she means well, but she all for it when I got some drama going on. When I called her and told her about my promotion at the hospital, she gave me a dry ass, *"Oh, that's nice,"* but let me go on a rant about Gavin and me; she all for the shits then. I never understood a person that simply cannot be happy for another person's success. So rather than be happy, they make a point of exposing a flaw in that person. Hating, the result of being a hater is jealousy. The hater doesn't really want to be the person he or she hates. The hater wants to knock someone else down a notch 'cause it has gotten to them emotionally, and they don't know no other way to handle the fact you are doing just fine, happier in whatever you're doing and how you're doing it. So, they speak about you to others, or in Lexi's case, she goes straight to social media like they give a damn about her in real life. That's the kicker. Alexis is always griping about something, and I was tired of it.

"Misery loves company, Love, but I can't have none, so she better go on and find a new playdate."

"Well, if you really feel that way, then talk to her, tell her how you feel, and maybe y'all can come to an understanding of some sort," she suggested, handing me a strand of hair.

"Yea, maybe," I said, now looking down at the message that had just come through my line.

"Earth to Sage," Love sang, snapping her fingers in my face.

I sat silently as I continued to make large triangular parts. I hated braiding Love's hair. We would spend more time talking than I did braiding, making it an all-day project. I interlocked the honey blonde extensions into her hair and braided swiftly while venting my ass off, moving quicker than normal. I had one last row, and I was home free.

Taking a deep breath, I decided to let Love in on the bigger issue at hand. "I have a problem, Love, and it's way more complicated than a dry ass subliminal Facebook post."

"Oh, I already knew that. You ain't never been one to be pressed about the opinions of others. So, what's this really about, Sage?"

I closed my eyes and wondered what "normal" life looked like. I couldn't identify with normality, which most of the time I was ok with. Hell, I was made to stand out. But in a world full of the "norm," I felt more and more alone at times like this. I looked down at Love and didn't want to rub my shit off on her. I watched as she texted, kissing emoji's and chuckled in-between messages. She was in a whole 'nother headspace and finally at peace. So, me bringing her into my world didn't feel right.

"Sage. It's not like you to be so uptight. Talk to me."

I took a deep breath and tossed back the cup of Patron before I laid it on thick.

"I think I found my daughter."

"What? Where? When? How?" She said, turning to face me.

"Be still, girl," I chortled, smacking my lips. I grabbed her shoulders and shifted her back to her initial position.

"I have a friend that had a friend, that had a friend, and they believe they found her file. She's been right here in Chicago the whole time, Love." I could feel myself getting emotional, so I took another breath, trying to play it cool. "She went off the map once she turned eighteen, and they lost track of her. But they think that they have located her again, and he is supposed to be bringing me her file when he returns to Chicago next week. They have pictures and everything. I don't even know where to begin. I mean, I have pictured how she may look and what part of me did she inherit. For twenty-two years, I have been walking around here sizing up every little girl that has walked through the clinic doors or rang me up in the department store. I don't know if I am ready for this, Love." I stared out the window in utter disbelief at how my life was beginning to unravel.

Here it was not one, but two men asked me for my hand in marriage. One with which I had connected on a level that I didn't even know existed. Another in which was the only man I had ever been with but could never connect with. Part of it is that I had held this dark secret from him for so long and....

"Oh my God, Love..." I said, clasping my mouth. "How am I going to tell Gavin that I may have found the daughter he never knew existed?"

"You just did," Gavin said, emerging from the back room.

Our Love Story is My Favorite

I GRIPPED SAGE'S LEG firmly after noticing Gavin was actually on a call and not listening in on our convo. For a second there, my heart stopped, and I was sure we were going to have to tag-team Gavin's big behind. It was no surprise that the man was on his phone; that Bluetooth was always in his ear, and that damn phone was glued to his hand twenty-four seven. Today was one of those days that I was glad he intervened, though. This was a conversation that really rubbed me the wrong way, and I hate going back and forth trying to solve Lexi and Sages' issues. The two of them had a love-hate relationship that could be heaven or hell if shit hit the fan. When it came to drama, I really ain't want no parts of it. I'm not anti-social or anything, and I don't mind helping people sort out their issues, but I sure as hell don't want to become part of the issue.

"Gavin, what are you doing here?"

"Well, it's nice to see you too, Sage," he teased. He walked over to Sage and put his lips against hers.

He slapped me on the back of my head playfully, making me bite my tongue and trying to trip his big ass.

"You missed," he teased, almost losing his balance.

141

Now, this caught me off guard because the Gavin I had known over the years was nowhere near an affectionate or playful fella. Now Sage had told me he could be a teddy bear, but I had never seen a compassionate bone in his body. The funny thing is, when a man knows for sure you ain't gone put up with his shit no more, his tune changes, and he tries to do a 360. But little do they know when a woman is done; that's just it. The fact that Sage had already started something new, she wasn't going back. If I didn't know anything about Sage, I knew that once she put her heart into something, there was no turning back. No matter how much Gavin tried, he had lost her. Now the hard part was her walking away. She always used the fact that he took care of her and put her through medical school as a reason behind her staying, but I knew it was more profound. One of the reasons was fear. Fear of letting go and having to do this all over again. No one liked starting over, but sometimes it can be the start of a whole new beginning. If anyone deserved to be loved right, it was damn sure Sage.

"Baby, I got some business to tend to at the new office, so I'll be out for a couple of hours, but I was wondering if I could take you to dinner this evening?' His baritone voice resounded as he grinned cleverly.

"I have to check my calendar." She played along, tugging at my hair.

"Be ready at eight. I won't ask again." He winked, making his way out the door.

Sage swung her legs over my head and went over to make sure the coast was clear.

"I won't ask again," she mimicked as we both laughed our ass off.

I pointed at her and twisted my lips. "One thing 'bout them tables...."

"They sholl do turn," we both said in unison with a smack of the lips and a high five.

"Heartache is by far one of the most painful things I have experienced in a lifetime. I mean, when you are in love, it seems like you can conquer the world, and when that goes crashing, so does the world around you. Everything appears to be going in slow motion, and no matter how much you try to speed it up, time never seems to be on your side." I closed my journal on that note. I was in utter disbelief that my life today was not the life I pictured it to be when I was sitting in that hotel room, balling my eyes out to K Michelle.

C.J. gripped my hand as I stared into the giant movie screen, popping the popcorn into my mouth like it was my last meal. I was two seconds away from ripping off this body shaper that had me snatched, might I add. I had convinced myself that C.J. liked his woman on the thick side because dealing with him, I put on a whole twenty pounds, and he loved every bit of it. He just doesn't know, I'm gone get it together ASAP, so he better hop on board with a sista.

"Wakanda Forever." The lady protested, making my heart smile. This *Black Panther* movie had my heart pumping the whole time. Not only was it an all-black cast, but it was finally something that didn't involve our people being beat and hung from a tree, a movie in which "the white man" was the minority. I just sat in awe, realizing that this is what Africa would have been. Without a European invasion. Not trying to go pro black on y'all, but this is our history.

Before I met Chris, I had never even thought twice about watching a damn Marvel movie. There were a lot of things I had never done before him. I had to learn how to let a man be a man with him, and I had no problem with that. I was just so used to taking the lead or settling for a brother that half stepped his way through our "situation."

TY NESHA

"Girl, if you don't let me hold this door…. or let me push ya chair in, woman." He had to fight me just to treat me like a lady. I learned with him that chivalry hadn't died. I just chose to give CPR to brothas that couldn't even see past the bare minimum. Out of all the heartaches and pain I had felt in my days, C.J. and I had a bond that wasn't like the rest. Hell, he wasn't even my type; I was so over my type. I learned that everything was a choice, and I chose the type of men I allowed into my life. I knew that if C.J. and I ever went our separate ways, it was meant for me to see that there are men out here that are willing to put back the broken pieces and make you forget your heart was ever broken. All you gotta do is stop re-reading all the old stories, open another book and try a new genre. This story was unfamiliar, but I was eager to keep turning the pages and writing a new chapter. After all, our love story is my favorite.

144

No Turning Back

"Let me get the Jerk nachos with extra sauce, no onion, and an Italian ice...."

"Damn girl, yo greedy ass gone order up the whole spot. Leave room for a brotha."

"I already ordered your food, lil ugly. Three jerk tacos coming about..."

"3 Jerk tacos, one nacho, and...."

"Now," I said over my shoulders, walking up to the cashier.

"Look at that, looking out for a brutha, huh? Bestie luh me?" Saint joked, throwing one of his arms over my shoulder, pulling out a wad of big faces.

I raised my eyebrows skeptically. "What the hell you been doin' and why you flodging?" I asked, crossing my arms as he paid for our food.

"Man, ain't nobody gotta stunt, lil bald head girl. I'm just trying to treat my ace to a meal. But lay off on the third degree, ya feel me," he countered, grabbing our food. I looked down momentarily, noticing the fresh pair of J's on his feet for the third time this month.

"I bet Mike loves yo' ass, huh?"

"Mike?" He asked, perplexed, his face was all twisted.

"Yea, Mike. As many of his shoes yo' ass rock, I'm sure you pay that man's whole mortgage damn near." I laughed.

"Yea, yo' ass laughing now. But, any time I cop you a pair, you take 'em with no hesitation."

"Duh, my guy. I ain't never one to turn down a pair of fly kicks." I hunched my shoulders nonchalantly.

He looked over his shoulders before he pulled open the door to his all-white Range and placed the bag on the seat. I hated that we always had to be all extra cautious in these streets. I just wanted him to know how it felt to be free from all that "gotta watch ya back" living. Saint got his money the best way he knew how, as if he had other options in the first place. His trifling ass mama had different men in rotation on a regular. That's all she ever gave a damn about. He was forced into the system at age nine because she was always strung out on that shit. Over the years, he dealt with DCFS, in and out of court, bouncing from family member to family member. To go along with that, the broken promises from his mom had his head so messed up, which in turn led to certain feelings towards women. All he wanted was his mom, but he felt his mom didn't want him. I couldn't even imagine how that could feel.

Saint and I have been best friends since I was twelve. Being that he was two years older than me, he always tried to play the big brother role. No matter what I went through, he was always there for me, whether he agreed with it or not; he had my back and called me out on my shit. He is the main reason why my trust for these clowns was obsolete. He showed me the game and told me to always be two steps ahead. Even though I was too stubborn to listen most times, I always made sure to stay on top of my shit.

I waited patiently as he talked shit over the phone to one of his homies. Saint had upgraded big time from that dusty

146

little boy that got a kick outta fighting and raising hell. Here he was leaning against his ride, all GQ smooth with a fresh lining, looking like Larenz Tate's long-lost son.

Saint has always been so guarded that he never let a female get close enough to him to get his heart. He had it set in his mind that he was incapable of receiving love. He didn't believe a female could love him cause his mom didn't. All he cared about was getting money, and no matter how much of a womanizer he was, women would fall putty at his hands. He would talk these females out of their best friend's panties, and they would stand in line and let him. To outsiders, Saint was as grimy as they came and he ain't give no fucks. He would interchange females by the day, but I knew the real Saint. The Saint that wrapped his Jersey around my waist when I started my period in the middle of the school day wearing an all-white skirt. The Saint that cried at the end of *Love and Basketball* and the Saint that slept at the edge of my bed and listened to me cry myself to sleep after my first heartbreak. We had so much history, and he was the only man that never asked me for anything more than to be who I was at all times and vice versa. There was nothing that could come in between us, which made these bitches hate me. But, they knew I wasn't one to play games, and as long as they knew what it was, my motto remained; do no harm, but take no shit.

By the time Saint and I had got to his spot, I was full and exhausted. I spread across his bed, taking up all the space while I flipped through the channels.

"Thank you," he said, snatching the remote out of my hand.

"Ugh, you already know my cable won't be on til next week. This the only time I get to watch the new episodes." I blew in frustration.

"Don't nobody wanna watch *Love and Hip Hop* all the time, especially when they get to see it live on a regular." He hinted, raising his brow and plopping down next to me.

I rolled my eyes and smacked my lips. "Speaking of which, I have something to tell you."

"Awe shit, what now?"

"I'm pregnant…" I mumbled under my breath.

I could see the steam emerge from his head as silence filled the room. He let out an exasperating breath. "I can't do this no more, Lex," he said calmly.

"Do what?" I snapped in agitation.

"I can't keep watching you carry yourself like you less than what you are. You already know I don't speak too much on you and that ole man, but damn girl. You out here playing yourself. You think this baby gone make him leave his ole lady? Don't answer that. A baby ain't gone change a damn thing," he said through gritted teeth. I remained silent to avoid blowing up on his ass.

He pulled me up and into him. I tried to resist, but he overpowered me, or I gave in, one or the other.

"You are too damn beautiful, dope, fly, and sexy to be settling for another female's seconds. You are and always will be a winner in my eyes. I always told you, you gotta stop jumping across oceans for a man that wouldn't step in a puddle for you." The look on Saints' face was so sincere that it scared me.

"You know it was always hard for me, Saint. I went through my whole high school years not knowing how it felt for guys to be on my heels. I never understood why they…"

"Because they knew better, Lex. That's why," he snapped.

"What?" I asked in confusion.

Saint turned to face me. "I spent all that time trying to keep them jokers off you because I knew that none of them would ever be cut enough to fill the shoes necessary for your kind," He confessed.

I didn't know if I should be pissed or flattered.

"You are so much more than this, so much more, Alexis Monroe." He grabbed my chin and lifted my eyes to his. I could feel the goosebumps begin to surface as he wrapped his arms around me. "I love you, Lex," he professed. "But I won't stand here and keep watching you do this to yourself."

I inhaled deeply and wiped the tears that had appeared out of thin air from my face. I kissed my best friend on the forehead. "I understand, and you don't have to watch anymore. I'll save you the trouble and let you watch me walk away instead." The sincerity in his face changed to a look of disgust. I knew at that moment that I had just become the epitome of the woman he despised the most. I headed towards the door, knowing that once you turn your back on a man like Saint, there is no turning back.

Saint would never understand that one of the most complex decisions a woman in love has to make is to either cut off a man who she's deeply in love with because he isn't treating her right or to proceed to love him and be devoted to him after the hurt, lies, and humiliation. Every woman isn't built to just walk away, but every woman ain't built for stayin' either.

A Jealous Friend is More dangerous than a Hateful Enemy

I HADN'T EVEN GOT in my office good before Dom came storming in behind me.

"So, when were you planning to tell me you were fucking this Love Wright?" Dom hissed as he slammed the door behind him.

"Man, I think you better lower your tone," I shot back dismissively.

Dom paced back and forth. I could feel the steam coming from his body. I acted as if I didn't notice, but it didn't take a rocket scientist to know he wasn't in a good headspace at the moment.

I remained cool to test his temperature, see where things go now that he has some new information. See, I like social trials because despite what people say, certain situations will reveal your character. I don't care what is said; if you got courage in your heart, you would be courageous during tough times. If you got pussy or coward in your heart, the right situation would bring out the pussy in you. You can't escape human nature! As for me, I'm a savage at heart, and so was Dom. My circle remains small for a reason. I learned that the snakes are not the ones that hiss behind you. They are usually slithering right where you can see them in plain sight.

150

"You said you had something for me?" I asked, clearing my throat.

"C.J., this is all bad, man," he confirmed as the sweat pebbles began to beam on his forehead.

"You told me you were just watching her, seeing what she knew. You did not say you would be fucking her!" He yelled, banging his fist on my desk.

Before he could utter another word, I pulled my piece from my waist and pressed it against his temple.

"I asked you to lower your tone," I said through clenched teeth.

Dom put his hands up in a non-defensive manner. "You got it." He nodded.

"Don't you think I know that, Dom? Don't you think I know?" I asked pompously.

I could see the hurt in his eyes, and I couldn't say I blamed him. I knew deep down the real one that was wrong was me. I knew better than to stick my hand in the cookie jar, but curiosity got me, and I folded. I lowered my gun and placed it back into its holster. Before I knew it, Dom had yoked me up so fast and threw me against the wall. Dom and I had fought many times before, and each time, one of us got the best of the other. Dom had me on weight and strength, but I was swift on my feet and calculated. If either of us let our guard down, it was over.

"Fool, I put my job at risk for you," he said through clenched teeth. "Everything on the line for you, and yo' bitch ass gone up a pistol on me. Next time you pull that muthafucka out, I suggest you use it," he hissed.

"It ain't like that man."

"Well, what's it like then?" He asked.

"It wasn't supposed to go this far, and..."

"Fuck all that. You need to dead that shit ASAP. If you don't, I will. I will take you in myself if I have to," He threatened. I knew damn well he would never do such a thing, even though he seemed damn convincing at the moment. We knew that if shit blew up, he was going down with me.

"Just give me more time, Dom."

"Time?" He asked, raising his brow. "So, what, you thinking 'bout telling her?"

There was a brief silence in the room. "Does she know anything? Remember?"

"She doesn't even talk about it, Dom. You would think the situation never happened. There is not a reminder in sight either," I concluded, shaking my head.

Dom was like the brother I never had, and I knew better than to ever pull a piece out on him. I was allowing my situation to cloud my judgment, and I knew better than this. Dom was from the streets for real; he just happened to be one that got away and joined forces with the "OPPS." He figured *if you can't beat 'em, join 'em.* And keeping him on my team taught me a lot. Many folded, and he wasn't one of 'em. He wouldn't dare let me call him a friend; we were brothers. He'd always say, *"You gotta watch these cats you call ya friends. You better than them, you smarter, and they know it. A jealous friend is more dangerous than a hateful enemy."*

Dom let his hands relax, but not his guard.

I buried my hands in my face and tried to think how I let this get so far. I knew better than to get entangled back up in this lifestyle. One wrong move, one wrong mistake can be a vicious game changer. His eyes still trained on me, he asked, "Is that the gun?" nodding in the direction of my desk.

"Nah, Tae got rid of it right away."

"Good, because that gun has a body on it, and if it ever surfaces and your fingerprints are pulled, they are going to bury you right next to your father, and you will be reunited wit' yo wife."

My heart sank as his words slapped me in my face so hard I wanted to strike back. I hurled over in pain, winded from the ugly truth.

"Some things are just better left alone, C.J. You opened this can of worms, now you gotta clean this shit up." Dom exited my office, leaving me in deep thought.

I trailed behind him five minutes later. I watched as he pulled into traffic. He gave me a head nod and a knowing grin. The sound of the screeching tires and blaring horn startled us both before the large 4 by 4 sent my friend's unmarked car spinning in circles and flipping it upside down.

Desiree

Love Don't Live Here No More

"Do you take this woman to have and to hold…" The pastor's words were music to my ears.

My dress, the ceremony, the venue, the faces of the guests—all of it was only something you could only dream about. It's only one day, and although I know it will whizz by, I wanted to savor every moment. I was never the little girl who envisaged a fairy tale wedding. If it were up to me, I'd opt for elopement. The sun shone through the church's atrium windows. Just as we were about to speak our vows, I looked up at my soon-to-be husband. I inhaled deeply, taking a moment to really let this day sink in. I thanked God for this moment. It was like no one else was here, just him and me. I refused to allow anyone in the room with me, not even….

"Till death do us part," he said before looking back up at me. I tried to pull away, but he gripped me tighter.

"Dontae?"

Where did he come from? Where was Kane?" I thought as my head spun in circles.

I felt a piercing pain in my stomach. Dontae had a repulsive grin spread across his face as I put my hand on my stomach. The wetness soaked into my hands, causing me to look down. My beautiful white dress was now saturated with blood. The steeple bell began to ring. I stood in terror as he counted all 12 chimes.

The loud thump startled me. I looked around in terror.

"Desiree, you good, baby girl?" Kane stood over me with his hand extended. I shook my head from side to side, declining his assistance. He sat next to me and wrapped his arms around me, pulling me into him.

"You just rolled out the bed, woman; sleeping all wild and shit. I'm just gone invest in some floor cushion. That way, next time, you won't make such a loud thump," he teased.

I rubbed my head embarrassingly. Kane kissed my forehead tenderly, easing any distress I had been left with. I assumed that after all of the time that had passed, all my fears would be erased. I could just move forward and break free. Tonight, I realized that no matter how far away from him I got, he still held me captive mentally, and here I was, dying to break free.

I walked into the bar with attentiveness, turning heads every which way. I spotted him in the back of the room as he flirted with the bartender. Once he spotted me, he shoo'ed her off, bringing her attention in my direction. She shot me the dirtiest look, 'causing me to smile inwardly.

Women were always intimidated by me. They don't like me 'cause I walk with so much confidence that you can't tell me shit. I had lost that. I hadn't felt this way in a while. They had no clue that when I was younger, I was told that I was trifling, I wasn't gone be shit... too damn black to ever find a man that would look at me twice. I was deemed less than by my own people because my melanin shade wasn't light enough, and although I was "cute for a dark skin girl," I had to work extra hard to pave the way for myself in the industry. Taking L after L until I was left to turn all my L's into lessons literally, everything they thought I was gone be, I proved them wrong. Today, you got bitches tryna get kissed by the sun daily to look like me; irony!

I slid the papers across the table. I studied him thoroughly. His eyebrows were already naturally arched, and he was always walking around with them crumpled up.

"Are you sure you wanna do this?"

The civility in his tone shocked me. This was the first time I had met with him alone since the altercation. Every time we met, it was arranged through our attorneys. It had been months since I had filed the papers for separation, and it seemed like he was finally accepting what was to come.

I thought about how I was always pulled in by his slick tongue and twisted meanings. I treaded lightly here and stood firm on my stance in this meeting. I waited to see if I felt something, anything, but it was evident; love doesn't live here anymore. It was nothing more than an abandoned building left to rot away from never-ending reminders and painful memories.

I nodded my head in confirmation. Dontae sighed as he resentfully signed the papers and pushed them back to me. I reached for the documents, and he placed his hand on mines.

"I'm sorry," he said sincerely before excusing himself and exiting the building.

My mouth parted, and a breath escaped me; a tear of joy trickled down my face. I scurried out of the bar anxiously to get back to the one man that showed me that *"love is indeed an act of courage, not of fear."*

It took me no time to get back to Kane. I don't even remember the drive here. All I know is I was ready for this ride with no seatbelts and no limits. The closer I got to the door, the harder the butterflies tapped dance inside me.

Love Chose Me

The retreating footsteps from a group of children walking down the road startled me. Moments later, a large shadow appeared from behind the condo.

"You really thought it was gone be that simple, doll?" He sneered.

I stared into his eyes, refusing to recoil. *I knew it was too good to be true,* I thought to myself. I refused to run as he walked closer toward me. He leaned into my ear and grabbed my jaws.

"I saw you fucking him," he whispered into my ear. My eyes broadened. Get yo' shit, and let's go."

I snatched away from him. "I'm not going with you, Dontae. Can't you see it's over. I have started over!"

"You know I hate repeating myself, Desi," he said through clenched teeth. "Now, I already gave you a pass with what you did to me. Don't you know I'm still healing from that shit?" He said, raising his shirt. "I figured that will make us even, and we can start fresh. But nooooooo, yo' ass done got pregnant. You definitely got this shit fucked up," he jeered, grabbing my face.

I pulled against my restraint, and he squeezed my jaw tightly. The murderous expression in his face caused my heart to shatter, knowing this was the end and there was no other way out. He shoved me to the floor, causing me to bang my head against my car.

"I didn't want it to come to this, but you leave me no choice," he said, picking me up and throwing me over his shoulders.

"Please put me down," I pleaded.

"Your wish is my command," he sang before snatching my keys out of my hands, throwing me into my trunk, and slamming it shut.

157

Alexis

Sorry Not Sorry

"*Alexis* Monroe, you got five more minutes, and I'm busting down that bathroom door."

"*Ok, ma, I'm almost finished!*" I screamed over Kelly Rowlands, *Motivation*. I popped my flavored strawberry bubblegum as I swayed my hips to the music, mouthing the lyrics. I brushed my bang over my forehead and braided the remainder of my hair in two French braids. It was my first day of high school, and I had no other choice but to be fly, being that summer had treated me well, blessing me with hips and breasts that were made for a grown woman.

The loud bang made me drop my mascara brush on my all-white crop top.

"*Dammit. Now I gotta change!*" I spat, snatching open the bathroom door.

"*Ok ma, hands up, don't shoot dang,*" I teased, walking towards the smell of bacon, eggs, and grits on a Monday morning.

"*You know, you know how to make me…. Ma?*" I whispered as I stood in the kitchen in shock as my mother's body lay stiff.

"*Ma!*" I screamed as I rushed over to her body, shaking her and smacking her face.

"Ma! Wake up, ma! Please, wake up." I sobbed over her body between chest compressions and mouth to mouth that I learned in summer camp.

"911, what's your emergency?"

"Helloooooooooooo, m'aam."

"Damn, you ain't gotta yell. I hear you!" I snapped, rolling my eyes as I walked up to the funny-looking teller.

"I'm sorry, ma'am. We have a pretty long line and…"

"Would you cut the ma'am shit? I ain't that old," I countered, sliding her my documents and identification.

"Do you have an account with us, Ms…?"

"Harris. Alexis Harris," I spoke slowly so she could understand 'cause she acted like she ain't see the shit in big, bold letters. "Nah, I don't have an account here."

The teller looked at me suspiciously as she ran the check through the machine for the third time.

"Is there a problem?"

"Well, it looks like this check can't be verified and…"

"Wait, what?"

"Ma'am, you may need to take it back to the person that issued it and find out what happened because it's not clearing in our system."

"I have been coming to this bank and cashing this check every month for the past four years. So, somebody got some explaining to do."

"Matter of fact, can you please tell Mr. John Harris he has a visitor," I demanded, snatching my check back.

"I'm sorry, Mr. Harris is a very busy man, and he goes by appointment only. I can take your…"

I slammed my fist down on the desk so hard I could've sworn the whole damn bank shook. "Tell Mr. Harris his daughter is here, and she is about to raise hell in less than sixty seconds if he doesn't pencil me in, in thirty."

My father buried his head into his desk and did everything possible to avoid looking up at me.

"I see you still running around here acting like a ghetto hood rat," he jolted, clearing his throat.

"You really are a sick individual, you know that?" I hissed, snatching the papers from under his nose." He gave me a nonchalant glare as he took a long sip from his cup.

"It's one thing that you let me get caught up in the system because you were too damn weak to raise your only daughter after the death of your wife. But to cut off my means of income, that's just really low down, don't you think?"

"Listen, I don't have time to get into this little self-pity party you put on every time you don't get what you want. I got a letter from your school stating that you were dropped from the program due to attendance, which means your money stops there. No school, no money. That was our deal, Lex. Sorry not Sorry, sweetheart," he grinned maliciously. "Oh, and by the way, I didn't *let* you get caught into the system, Alexis. You have yourself to thank for that. Your mother and I gave you everything that you needed, and instead of being grateful, you, in turn, became a self-centered little girl that walked around here like the world owed her diamonds, like she shitted out rose pedals on a regular."

"Really? That's funny because the last time I checked, the only one that felt like they were entitled to anything was you. You never gave a rat's ass about me, and when mommy died, you shut me out like I was some kind of stray, and you were my savior."

My father rose from his seat and chuckled cynically. "I promised my wife that I would keep her secret until you were old enough to know the truth. I spared your feelings for long enough, but today is the day that you will find out the real truth."

Confusion overcame me as I folded my arms across my chest. "What are you talking about, Dad?"

He stroked his chin and walked over towards me, sitting at the corner of the desk. "Lexi, I am not your father," he spat viciously.

"Wha... whattt...?" I said shockingly. I jolted from the chair, knocking it to the floor.

"It's one thing for you to be a piece of shit, but you will not bring my mother down with you with your lies," I hissed, causing a commotion as tears streamed down my face. One thing I hated was for anybody to see me cry. I'm far from a weak-ass cry baby that can't keep her emotions in check, but I was beyond pissed, and I wanted to strangle this man where he stood.

"Oh no, my dear. I loved your mother dearly, and I had nothing but the utmost respect for her and what she stood for."

"How so if you are accusing her of stepping out on you and having a baby?" I retorted, wiping my face ragefully.

"I never said such a thing, Lexi."

I was filled with confusion once again. "So, what are you saying?"

He shoved the papers into my chest. "I'm saying. My wife......" Either his words fell silent, or my ears fell deaf, drowning him out.

My heart beat rapidly as I watched his mouth move. My eyes shifted from his mouth back to the papers. I charged at him, pounding my fist into his chest. How could he be so

161

cruel? How could he make up such harsh things about my mother? Everything around me began to spin. I could feel my body give way. My body fell limp, and my eyelids became heavy as I gasped for air.

"Call an ambulance." Were the last words I could hear before everything else faded into darkness.

Dontae

Trapped

"Dontae, wait up..."

I threw my football gear over my shoulder and kept walking, picking up my speed at the sound of Malcolm's voice.

"I can't talk right now, man. I got somewhere to go," I said over my shoulders, making my way through the boy's locker room.

"Wait," he said, grabbing my shoulder and turning me towards him.

"What happened in there last night?" He asked, giving me an instant migraine.

"I don't know what you talking about, man. I told you, I got shit to do." I grimaced, slapping his hand off my shoulder. We paused for a minute as a few of our other teammates passed us by.

"So, now you wanna pretend like last night didn't happen? Well, it did." He glared.

I pulled him to the side and began to talk in a whispered tone. "Look, I'm not that way. I... I..."

"You what, Dontae? You walk around here like a playboy of the century, thinking having two or three women on your arm is going to be a front for who you really are. No matter how many women you sleep with, you will forever be searching for who you really are in them. Like, why not come to terms and accept it? You are...."

Before he could finish his statement, I gave him a quick shot to the jaw, knocking him cleanout.

163

TY NESHA

"Stay out my way, faggot," I hissed before stepping over him.

By the time I had gotten home, I couldn't hold it any longer. The words played in my head repeatedly. I hated myself for what I had done to Malcolm, but I couldn't let him mess up my life right now. Things were going so well and....

"NaNa, can I talk to you for a min?"

"It gotta be fast, Dontae. Mama got a hot date tonight," she said, doing a little shimmy. She was always happier when she had a date or guest over.

"Nana, I really need to..."

"How much?"

"What?"

"How much you need, and what's her name?" She asked, having it all wrong.

"I know you saw last night," I said. She stopped in her tracks and started to pick up around the kitchen. Whenever my nana got upset, she would clean even if there was nothing to clean. This was her way of not dealing with the actual issue at hand.

"Nana, please. I'm different. Things are different. Don't you see it? None of the girls are good enough. They don't make me feel...."

"Listen here," she said, shaking me. "I don't want to hear anything else about what you think you are. It's a faze, baby, and it will pass. You are a handsome young man, and there ain't a girl in this city that isn't dying for you to make them yours." She smiled. "Now, I'm going to call Pastor Poole and see if we can get a session for him to pray over you and this demon that is trapped inside you trying to attack your mind 'cause I'm not having it."

"Let me out, Dontae. Please, please! I feel sick. You can't do this... please," Desi pleaded, interrupting my thoughts, banging on the trunk.

She hated being confined and enclosed in any way possible. When she was younger, her psychotic ass mama used to lock her in the closet for hours for any reason she saw fit. I

164

chuckled at the thought of Ms. Kennedy's fine ass. She and I had been fucking for over five years, and her ass would do anything I told her to do. It took nothing for me to get the information on Desi out of her. Some good dick and charm took me a long way. That's what tickled me about women. They were so damn desperate for love that they would do anything to get and keep a man, even if he belonged to someone else. I watched my mother go from a strong, daring, articulate college professor to a desperate, conniving insecure woman at the hands of a man to the point where she would turn on her only child. I spent most of my childhood trying to figure out who this shell of my mother had become and why she didn't fight just as hard for her son as she would for a man that didn't give two shits about her.

I pulled up to the abandoned building and lit a square before making a call. I took a long pull and thought about how this was all going to play out.

By the time I got Desi into the building, she was sweating profusely, and blood was seeping through her skirt. I tied her to the chair and put the phone to her ear.

"K...K...Kane," she said calmly over the phone. She took a deep breath and closed her eyes.

"What's up, baby? You good? I have been calling you all night. Where you at?"

"Kane, I can't do this anymore. I need some space right now."

"What? Girl quit playing. Where you at?"

"I'm not playing Kane. I need you to hear me. I got an abortion today, this morning. Me and Dontae are going to work things out. We...."

"You killed my baby? Desi, don't make me act a fool, man. This shit ain't no joke and I ain't finna play..."

"I ain't playing. Being with you made me feel trapped. I don't like to feel like I can't breathe and move at my own leisure. I'm sorry, but it's over, Kane." Dontae snatched the phone and ended the call.

"Dontae, if you ever had an ounce of love for me, you would let me go. Please, something isn't right and..."

"Shut up!" I retorted. I looked her up and down as her chocolate skin glowed a glow that I hadn't seen in years. *What had I done? Who in the hell was I?* I loved Desi, but I knew that I was no longer in love with her. This was all principle, and for her defiance, she had to pay. I poured her a drink and mixed up a little concoction to assist her with her pain.

Walking over to her, I could see the anguish in her face, but there wasn't an ounce of sympathy running through me.

"Here, take a sip," I said, putting the drink to her mouth. She clamped her lips tightly and shook her head from side to side. I squeezed her jaw tightly, prying it open. I shoved the cup into her face and poured the liquid down her mouth, forcing her to drink it.

I'll be damned if my wife brought another baby into this world that wasn't mines. I frowned before throwing the cup to the floor.

But there was one final thing that needed to be done before I made my exit.

It was only a matter of time before I could complete my job, so I decided to let her sit here for a while and think about her actions. My phone rang as I exited the building.

"C.J., what up?"

"It's Dom?"

"What? What are you talking about?"

"He..." There was a brief silence. "Meet me at Mercy? Now!!" He demanded before ending the call.

My Girl

I **MARCHED BACK AND** forth, trying to process this damn phone call. Now, I ain't no damn dummy, and I know damn well Desi wasn't crazy enough to go back with Tae. Or was she? This just wasn't adding up. She was happy, and she didn't even believe in....

"I need you to hear me, Kane; I got an abortion today, this morning." Her words replayed, and I remembered she and I had spent the whole morning and afternoon sleeping in.

"She was trying to tell me something." I cursed, grabbing my keys off the counter.

"Ayo Shawn, you still know how to ping a phone?"

"You know I do...I can do you one better, have you at the front door," he said arrogantly.

"Give me the info, and I'll have you a location five minutes, tops."

It took me less than 20 minutes to get to the address. "This can't be right," I said to myself before shutting off my engine. I sat outside the abandoned building, waiting for some sort of hint or inkling of where to start looking. There were no numbers on the building, and I ain't have time to go from the beginning to the end. I went around to the back and tapped lightly on the old wood, barely holding up against the hinges.

Before I could knock again, I heard a painful scream emerge from the building behind me.

Trying not to let anyone know I was in the area, I refrained from calling out to her. My heart beat against my chest as I dreaded what was happening to her behind those doors. Instinctively, I kicked in the door only to find Desi hurled over in a pool of blood.

"Desi, baby."

"The baby, Kane. He killed the baby!"

"Don't worry, baby. I got you. I'm so sorry, baby. I'm so sorry," I said as I untied her from the chair.

"He's not gone stop, Kane. He's not gone stop until he kills me," she sobbed before losing consciousness in my arms.

"I will always keep you safe."

"Mr. Wright?" A voice called out, bringing me back.

"Yes, that's me."

"Hello, my name is Doctor Vitale. Are you here with Desiree James?"

"Yes, sir, I am."

"Have a seat, son."

As soon as I spotted Dontae emerge from the double doors, my blood started rushing. The thought of ending him here and now put me in a trance. Glancing toward the waiting room, I made contact with who I needed to see. He nodded his head in acknowledgment, and I returned the service. Just as I got ready to make the call, I raised my hand, signaling a halt.

"C.J."

Damn. I cursed, trying to remain incognito. Spotting me, he made his way over, and Dontae's coward ass trailed behind him wearing a humorous grin.

"Kane, what brings you out this way?" C.J. asked, adjusting his suit coat. He wasn't his normal self, so I decided to play it cool just to test his temp.

"Yea, my girl just gave birth to my baby boy this morning. I just came out here to get a little air," I said, sensing the discomfort in Dontae's demeanor.

As expected, C.J. was shocked to hear the news.

"Whaaaat? You had a baby? Why didn't you tell me? You never said anything about your girl being pregnant…Or even that you had a girl?"

I shook my head. "Yea, I'm a pretty private person, and I always figured things and people will expose themselves at the right time," I said disdainfully.

At this moment, I was just about ready to buck, and if C.J. wanted to get it, then he could too. This clown needed to be dealt with, and I ain't have time to wait on Karma to fuck him up. I was gone play the Grim reaper today. I had got Desi to the hospital just in time to save the baby. Now she is in a coma, and my son is in an incubator fighting for his life. So, I ain't see no reason to be generous today.

"Well damn, congratulations," C.J. said, reaching out for a handshake. I paused briefly, my eyes fixed on Dontae.

"Well, tell the lucky lady?"

"Desiree," I said firmly, grabbing C.J.'s hand.

"Come again?" C.J. said, clearing his throat.

"Why the fuck you fucking around for? You trying to create drama, and this ain't the time for that Kane, we…."

"Calm down, my man. You preaching to the choir, but uh, bruh here… he got my girl in a coma and my son fighting for his life. So, I ain't tryna do shit. It's already done," I said, giving the signal. My goons surrounded C.J. and his brother. I couldn't care less about this fool status. His brother was a bitch and if he wanted to ride with 'em, then let that clown be his demise.

"Whoa, what the hell Kane? What you mean coma? What the fuck is he talking 'bout, Tae?"

Tae stood firm with his face all twisted. "Screwface ain't never lit no cigarette, homeboy," I told him, now walking in his direction. Just as Dontae thought it was sweet to buck up, I stole his ass, knocking him to the ground. C.J. tried to intervene, but I upped my pistol and put it right to his head.

"I like you and all, but not at the expense of my family." I cocked the gun.

"Kane, Nooooooooo!" My sister called out, pushing C.J. out the way.

Bangggggggggg!

4 years prior

"Kane, why is this baby crying so much? I don't know what else to do. She won't take her bottle, I changed her, I don't know."

"Calm down, Calm down. Let uncle take the wheel." I chuckled, taking the baby from Love's hands. Silence filled the room as my niece made cooing sounds.

"Why doesn't she do that with me?" Love cried, burying her hands into her face.

"Well, sis, she probably mad cuz you ain't name her yet."

"Shut up." She laughed, slapping me on my arm.

"I'm just playing, dang. Nah, sis, you gotta relax. Believe it or not, she can feel whatever stress you feel, and if you ain't right, it throws her off. Try again," I said, placing my niece into her arms.

Love grabbed her daughter and smiled for the first time since she had given birth. "You feel that?" I asked her.

"Yea, I do," she said, rocking her side to side. "I've got sunshine on a cloudy day."

170

"Ooh, ooh," I chimed in.

"I guess you say, what can make me feel this way… My girl." We both sang in harmony.

"Look, Kane, she is smiling."

Sage

Truth Be Told

D **OM AND I LAID** *across the blanket entangled into one another. His chestnut-brown eyes gazed into mines as I placed a strawberry into his mouth. His six-pack abs and pecs glistened under the sunlight peering onto us. He would often flexibly relax them, very content with his robust and agile build on full display, stirring my honey pot.*

"Dom, I need to tell you something," I said, taking a deep breath. Tears clouded my eyes. Deep inside, I knew that this was the man for me. He gave me everything that Gavin had failed to.

"If you not saying you gonna marry me, then there is nothing to discuss." He smiled. I stuck my finger into his right dimple and twisted it out of habit.

"You know I need to square away things with Gavin before I can make that commitment. I gotta end this the right way," I told him, leaning for a kiss. He turned his head away from my lips.

"Nah, you don't get these lips until…

The large bang from outside the hospital startled me. The alarm sounded as the emergency code from the speakers instructed all staff to stay inside of the building. I wiped the tears from my eyes and backed into one of the rooms. I didn't even realize someone was on the other side of the room. All I could see was their silhouette through the divider. The familiar

172

voice almost made me call out, but something inside me said, "*Be still*".

The talking on the phone grasped my attention as I walked closer to the direction of the voice. "What do you mean, Gavin? I'm sitting here in the hospital. They said the baby was in my tubes, and they have to do an emergency DNC… it's when…"

I pulled back the divider, enraged, ready to knock the shit out of Alexis. Lexi's eyes widened. Her mouth hung open as I reached out for the phone.

"Lexi baby, what are you saying?" His baritone brought butterflies to my stomach. Frozen, I couldn't believe what was going on.

"You slept with my man then looked me in the face repeatedly and called me your sister? Your friend?" I said through gritted teeth.

As I said it all aloud, it suddenly dawned on me that this is why she always had an attitude whenever shit was going good with Gavin and me. This is why she was so bitter and miserable towards me. How naïve was I? The signs had always been there. Alexis was always leaving the room whenever Gavin came, or Gavin would exit when Lexi arrived.

"I was with him before I even knew who you were," she sobbed, gasping for air.

"So that makes it better? You knew about me, sat in my house, wiped my tears when he didn't come home, when all along he was with you?"

"Sage…"

"Don't," I interrupted her, raising my hand.

"I'm so sorry!" Lexi cried, wiping her face with every tear that poured from her eyes.

The rage I felt turned to hurt and back to rage in a matter of seconds. I had become blinded by anger and lost in a sea of hurt. She was sobbing hysterically as snot and tears covered her face. The tears fell from my face without my permission. "How could you?" I wept.

Her eyes had begun to roll into the back of her head as her body jolted. She was convulsing, and I was too damn out of it to move my planted feet. I made my way over to her bed, calling in a possible code blue. I pulled her bang back so that I could get a better view of her eyes. I jumped back in disbelief as I was trying to gather what I had just seen. I tried to say something, but nothing came out. Speechless, I shook my head to the side.

"Noooo, Nooo. It can't be. This can't be true," I said, backing away from her. The staff rushed in, pushing me away. The room spun in complete circles as I curled into a corner in total shock.

I wrapped my arms around her and examined her little body, counting all five fingers and toes. Her dark curly hair stuck to her forehead. I pulled it back from her face, and she had the most unique birthmark beneath her hairline.

"My baby girl," I exhaled. "My baby girl."

I rubbed my fingers across her forehead. The shape of her birthmark was one I could never forget; it put me in the mind of the African Continent. A smile spread across her face.

"Look at that; she's smiling at the angel," the nurse said, placing her on my shoulder.

"Alright, times up." My mother barged into the room, back to her usual self.

"Wait, what?" I asked as she took my baby from my arms.

"Say goodbye because I'll be damned if you are going to make a fool outta me and bring a baby into my home at 14."

"Sage!" My coworker called out.

"How is she, Brit?" I asked. Here I was in the hospital with my boyfriend and Lexi at the same damn time. Dom slipped into a coma during his surgery, and from the looks of things, Lexi was going down the same road.

"Hanging in there. She sustained cardiac arrest in the abdominal radiology ward. But, the surgery was successful, and she is stable. She is in recovery. You can wait here in her room until she gets back."

"What happened?"

"Her gut was full of blood. One of her fallopian tubes ruptured, but they were able to successfully repair it. She is no longer pregnant."

I flinched. Her words pierced my soul.

"I'm sorry," she said as I hung my head down into my hands.

"If you don't mind me asking. What is her relation to you?"

I paused briefly, raising my head in slow motion. The words fought to emerge from my mouth. How did my life become such a fucking soap opera? Today was the day reality would come slapping me into my face, catching me completely off guard.

"Truth be told… she, she is my daughter."

The Bitter Truth

Dear Son,

If you are reading this letter, that means I am no longer alive, and I no longer have to carry the burden that has been weighing down on me for decades. I never really knew how to communicate with you verbally or even bond with you so that you can understand why I remained so tough on you and turned my head to the obvious. Truth is, I knew about your brother from the day he was conceived. I couldn't live with the actuality that came with having to face him. He was only a reminder of the hurt that I had endured during my younger years. Truth is….

My jaw dropped as I continued to read the letter. My heart sank into my chest as I tried to envision every word as if I were watching it happen right before my eyes.

"Listen, Elaine, we can't keep doing this. We can get in a lot of trouble and…"

"And what? I already told you there isn't any other option. We do things my way or…"

Elaine sat on the desk in her office with her legs parted just enough to inhale the sweet aroma. She was tempting, but this was all wrong. Elaine was ten years older than me, and her father was the head of the school board; he had complete control of my scholarship. I was only two classes away from finishing my degree when I met Dontae's mother, Elaine. She had her heart set on being with me, and I had my heart set

176

on being with your mother. She had been bribing me for months that she would not only tell your mother, but she would tell her father as well, risking not only my scholarship but, most importantly, my freedom. No court in their right mind would buy that I was the one that was genuinely being sexually assaulted, and Elaine played a damn good victim at that.

I had already told my father that I was willing to throw it all away to escape the torture and hold she had on me, but he told me to *"man up, it's only a little pussy"*. He would laugh and tell me that no boy or man in his right mind would turn down pussy no matter how it was being delivered to him. There was no such thing as a woman taking advantage of a boy or a man in a sexual way in his mind. I disagreed, but I knew that I had to do what I had to do. I had a chance to stop the cycle. I had a chance to fix it with you, and I didn't. I took you away from your mother to protect you from the monsters of the world when all along, I allowed the beast to invade my home. Instead of protecting you, I took on the role that my father had passed down to me and allowed my son to endure the same humiliation that I had to undergo, but worse. I kept repeating my father's words and figured that it would make you a better man in the future, but I was wrong. Not only did I walk away from my firstborn, but I had also wholly alienated my second. Please find it in your heart to forgive me, for I have learned that a brutal secret can be deadlier than the bitter truth.

As I sit here prepared to close my eyes after 12am, I reflect back on this past year. It was a hell of a storm that I had to endure, and I'm not fully out of it yet, but the days get brighter and brighter. I've lost many people I considered friends but gained friends that I now consider family. It hasn't been an easy year by far. I've taken countless losses, but I celebrate the wins I was blessed with. This past year, I've kept my sanity by constantly looking at the "silver lining" in any bad situation I was put in or put myself in. Humble pie was a regular meal that I had to eat. I say all of that to humbly say this; forget taking Ls and forget the constant beat down of life... This is the year of greatness, and the best of my yesterdays will be the worst of my tomorrows. I've fought the battles alone, and I have conquered situations ordinary people would crumble in. Today, I celebrate another year of life and many more chances to be great. Today is my birthright and a great fuckin day for a great fuckin man.

I closed my eyes and blew out the candles to my cake.

"Now, let's party!" Derek, the club bouncer, said, pointing to the D.J. Bruno Mars blared through the club, and the sound of bottles popping surrounded me. I laughed silently as I noticed Dontae and Jade huddled in the corner. I turned to my other side, and there was my right-hand man Kane and my sister, Desi. I gave them my blessing, raising my glass in the air. I sent one up for Dominick, wishing he was here.

Love emerged from her seat, catching everyone's attention as the lights dimmed and the spotlight hit us as she pulled me in the middle of the dance floor. She was the only one in gold, a sequined dress that fit her curvy body to perfection. Her braids were pulled up in a bun just the way I liked it, where I could see every feature her face possessed.

I stroked the side of her face and whispered into her ear, "All the stars couldn't shine like you on your worst day. You make everything all good," I assured her.

"And you make everything better," she crooned sweetly, biting my earlobe.

I kissed her lips sensually. Without warning, a feeling of culpability conquered me.

"Love, I need to tell you something."

"No, not tonight, C.J. Tonight is all about you," she whispered into my ear.

I wrapped my arms around her waist tighter and pulled her into me. "I love you, Love Wright," I whispered to her.

"I love you too, Christopher James." She smiled.

"Wait right here." I smiled cleverly as I headed over to the stage.

Love had a look of ambiguity on her face as I grabbed the mic and cleared my throat. All eyes were now on me.

"Don't worry, baby. I won't outshine you tonight." I winked, assuring Love that I wasn't going to embarrass her with my vocal skills.

Laughter and giggles filled the room before I spoke again. My eyes shifted towards the door as two detectives flashed their badge to Derek. They pushed their way through the crowd and stopped at the edge of the stage.

"Christopher James?"

"What's this about?" I asked as the detective nodded towards the other.

"I need you to step down. We have a warrant for your arrest."

"What?" I said, stepping down to face them.

"Christopher James, you are under arrest for the rape of Jade Butler."

"Oh hell nah! Are y'all serious?" I asked as my eyes shifted over to the award-winning Jade as she cried in the arms of what appeared to be another detective.

"You have the right to remain silent…

Follow your heart; But take your brain with

I STORMED INTO THE police station in an uproar. I
hadn't been here since...

"Ms. Wright, how nice to see you again?" Detective
Perry chirped, leading me into the precinct. I hated the CPS. I
scanned the room as the uniformed officers were scattering
every which way.

"I'm not sure about nice, Detective. You have my client
in custody, and I would like to know under what grounds you
are holding him?" I snapped, getting straight to the point.

"Your client?" He said, face twisted in confusion.

I had gone into lawyer mode, and I'll be damned if I was
leaving this place without Chris.

"Yes, *my* client," I confirmed, passing him my card.

"Let's just hold off on that. We have something else that
we would like to discuss with you."

"Such as?" I asked as he led me to the briefing room.

The door slid shut as a lady Detective crept in. Detective
Perry pulled out my seat.

"How *well* do you know Christopher James?" The lady
detective asked.

180

Love Chose Me

"Well enough to know he isn't a rapist, and I'll have you know as his attorney, I will represent him to the fullest," I said in a matter-of-fact tone.

"Hold fast there," The lady spoke again.

"And who are you?" I asked, annoyed that she hadn't even bothered to introduce herself, but she wants to know a timeline for myself and C.J.

"My apologies, this is Detective Banks, the Senior Investigating Officer in the case of the murders that went down a few years ago."

The overhead projector buzzed from its platform on the ceiling, and as Detective Perry pressed the clicker, a series of images came into view. His face was serious.

"We have you know that *your client* has a very extensive rap sheet. But I am sure you are aware of this being that you are his attorney," she said condescendingly, pushing over a file that belonged to C.J.

"Did he happen to tell you about the death of his wife?" Perry asked, pausing the video, showing the crime scene of a woman lying in a pool of blood.

"Wife?" I thought to myself, trying to keep it together.

"Where are you going with this Detective?" I asked, maintaining my composure, trying not to look at the screen.

Don't get me wrong. Inside, I was fuming. I shuffled through the file nonchalantly but quite surprised by the life Chris had led. They had pictures of him along with notes and documents that were in an attempt to pin him to a variety of murders, extortion charges, and so many other things. Why hadn't I done my research, and why is Chris's file tied to the restaurant shooting? Having enough, I took a deep breath and pushed the file back towards her.

She gave a trivial sneer. "But that's not what we are here to talk about," she added, pushing another file over that read,

181

Neveah Marie Nelson. I looked up at the projector, and my baby's face lit up to the screen.

"What is this?" I asked. "Why do you have this?" I questioned ragefully. "Why are you showing me this? This case is closed and...."

"Well, actually, it's been reopened."

"What do you mean reopened?"

"We all know that this was an accident. I didn't mean to do it. They cleared me, and I put it behind me. Why are we doing this again? I don't want to do this today," I said, breaking down.

It had been over two years, and I tried to push the vision, her face, and everything tied to that day to the back of my mind. I pushed out of my seat and walked up to the screen. A cascade of tears fell from my face against my own will as I outlined her face with my fingers. I was not ready for this. I was not trying to relive this horrifying scene.

The loud bang startled us all. We weren't sure if it was firecrackers or a gunshot as we all panicked looking for my baby girl.

"Where is she, Lexi? Why would you leave her?" I cried, searching for a hint of my daughter.

I trailed around the corner and leaped up the stairway, skipping steps on the way up.

I heard my daughter's voice.

"I want my mommy," she said as I reached the top.

"Love? It's nice that you decided to join us," my ex said cunningly.

"Give me my baby."

"Don't you mean our baby, Love?" He smiled, kissing Veah on the cheek.

Unconsciously, I pulled my gun from my apron, pulling back the clip. Ever since Tia's death, I never walked around naked. Thankfully, I never had to use it. In this case, it showed as my hands trembled while I pointed it at Neveah's father.

"What are you gone do with that, girl? We both know you scared shitless of guns," he teased.

"I'm not playing with you. Put her down now!" I bellowed.

"Ok, Ok, damn. A brotha can't even visit his child without being held at gunpoint nowadays," he countered, putting her down. Just as she was walking in my direction, the commotion from the room behind me startled me, causing me to drop my gun. The shot rang out as I watched my three-year-old baby girl fall motionlessly to the floor.

"Noooooooooooooooooooooo!"

"Unfortunately, we've never been able to make any of the cases stick, but the evidence against Chris today seems to be pretty compelling," the lady said, breaking me from my trance.

I furrowed my eyes in anger. "What? What evidence? What the hell are you talking about?" I asked, walking towards her.

She patted the chair next to her, keeping her voice low. "Ms. Wright, come take a seat." The briefing room at this police station was not the time or place for a reunion. It was my hell, and I wished that I could leave here and never look back.

I sat in the chair, feeling an aura in the air that told me I wasn't going to like what was to come.

"Well, Ms. Wright, there's new evidence that has surfaced. One of our officers had run a ballistics search on the bullet from the crime. New evidence shows that there was some sort of mix up and your gun was not the gun that matches the bullets and fragments from Neveah's death."

A sense of relief, as well as muddle, conquered me as my hands began to shake. "So, are you saying I did not kill my daughter?"

"No ma'am, you did not," the lady Detective spoke.

"Other evidence with the weapons of alleged suspects or others involved in a case of your daughter has linked the forensics to the bullet, which in turn is a perfect match."

I swallowed hard, throwing Detective Perry a sideways glance. "Wait, I don't understand." I inhaled, trying to find a calm place in this.

"What we are saying is, after placing *your client* into custody, we also retrieved a gun from his office."

As she spoke, I could feel the room closing in on me, suddenly making me nauseous.

"It appears that it wasn't your gun that killed your daughter. It was your client's. Christopher James." In that one statement, it felt as if every breath inside my body had sucked away.

"Is this some kinda joke?" I asked, jolting from my seat.

"No, it isn't," she said firmly, motioning for the officer to enter. The door slid open.

"Your client," she said cunningly, walking Chris into the room. My eyes filled with tears as he hung his head low.

The lady detective placed her hand on my shoulder and whispered, "Follow your heart, but take your brain with." Before she exited the room, closing the door behind them, leaving my heart to break into pieces as I stood in front of the man that went from being the gentleman of my dreams to the devil in my worst nightmare in a matter of seconds.

CPSIA information can be obtained
at www.ICGtesting.com
Printed in the USA
LVHW020257280721
693844LV00007B/944